Also by Paul Stewart

THE THOUGHT DOMAIN
THE WEATHER WITCH

Paul Stewart

ADAM'S
-ARK-

Illustrated by Kevin Jones

PUFFIN BOOKS

To Jane

PUFFIN BOOKS

Published by the Penguin Group
Penguin Books Ltd, 27 Wrights Lane, London w8 5TZ, England
Penguin Books USA Inc., 375 Hudson Street, New York, New York 10014, USA
Penguin Books Australia Ltd, Ringwood, Victoria, Australia
Penguin Books Canada Ltd, 10 Alcorn Avenue, Toronto, Ontario, Canada M4V 3B2
Penguin Books (NZ) Ltd, 182–190 Wairau Road, Auckland 10, New Zealand

Penguin Books Ltd, Registered Offices: Harmondsworth, Middlesex, England

First published by Viking 1990
Published in Puffin Books 1992
1 3 5 7 9 10 8 6 4 2

Text copyright © Paul Stewart, 1990
Illustrations copyright © Kevin Jones, 1990
All rights reserved

The moral right of the author has been asserted

Printed in England by Clays Ltd, St Ives plc
Filmset in Palatino

PART
ONE

—1—
THE WRONG DIAGNOSIS

Had it not been for Oscar, there is every likelihood that Adam would never have learned to communicate at all. Locked in the secret world he had retreated to so young, he steadfastly refused to acknowledge the loving smiles of his parents, ignored their patient, or otherwise, words of encouragement, and squirmed and writhed in their arms fretfully whenever they picked him up. His apparent rejection of the two people he depended on made them feel awful, of course, but there was something even worse than any of this behaviour. The screaming. For no reason that either his mother or his father could determine, their tiny son would bellow and wail furiously until his face was blue and his throat was red raw.

"Adam, Adam, Adam," his mother would whisper into his ear, hugging him tearfully close as she tried in vain to calm him down. But the screeching, sobbing and desperate flailing around would continue until, at last, exhaustion overcame him. Then, his limbs would go limp, his eyelids would grow heavy, and finally, finally a look of peace would smooth away the troubled expression on his face as he fell asleep.

"Little angel," his mother would say, smoothing his hair down and covering him up with a blanket. "My little frightened angel."

She would look at him one more time, just to check that he really was sound asleep, before going into the kitchen to make herself a cup of coffee. And sitting there with her hands wrapped round the warm mug, she would ask herself for what seemed like the millionth time, what had gone wrong with Adam. Sometimes she blamed herself — she *must* have done something wrong, although she hadn't a clue what. Sometimes she blamed her husband and they would quarrel about how cold he could be, how distant, how intolerant. At other times it was the doctors she would rail against, angry at their inability to help her and her son. And occasionally, very occasionally, it was Adam himself whom she accused. How could that beautiful bundle she had first held in the hospital ward have turned out anything other than perfect? What had happened to her baby?

Adam had been born at the end of May. Four days later, and weighing seven pounds nine ounces, he was driven home for the first time, all wrapped up and cradled in his mother's arms. When Miriam and Derek Williams had set off for the hospital they had been a couple. Now, a hundred or so hours later, they were returning a family.

May that year had been a particularly cold and wet month, but on the day Adam was born the sun had begun to get the upper hand and, as the summer slipped into gear, it was to prove the hottest on record. Even in the shade under his parasol and bonnet, the sun seemed to get through, turning the baby's soft skin a golden brown and bleaching his hair. As he lay in his cot, gurgling happily and gazing into space with his wide blue eyes, Miriam was sure she had never ever seen a more wonderful baby.

It wasn't long, however, before she began to notice that something was not quite right. The summer gradually cooled down and the leaves turned yellow and red. Then one night a severe gale stripped the trees completely and suddenly winter had arrived. Miriam tried to convince herself that everything was proceeding normally with her son, but she had read too many books on a baby's development to kid herself. Adam had reached the age where her voice and face should have evoked some kind of response, some kind of recognition.

But there was none.

When she reached down into the cot, he never made himself ready to be picked up. And when she took him in her arms, he would lie there awkwardly, never snuggling down comfortably. While no matter how she spoke or sang to him, he would remain aloof and indifferent to her.

"I just don't understand," she said to Derek. "There's something . . ."

But her husband didn't want to hear. If there was anything wrong with his son, then he would have nothing to do with it. He told Miriam that the problems were all in her head, that if she would just leave the baby alone a bit more he'd be fine.

Miriam held her tongue, but couldn't stop worrying. Finally, without telling Derek what she was about to do, she went to see the doctor, who sent her to the hospital, which put her in touch with a specialist who confirmed what she had suspected all along. The word the woman at the paediatric clinic had used was 'autistic', and though

9

Miriam didn't really know what it meant, she shuddered nervously at the realization that whatever was wrong with Adam, there was a medical name for it.

From that moment on things at home were somehow both better and worse. Better, because it was a relief to find out that she hadn't been imagining things and, as she learnt more about his condition, she was able to cope with his peculiar behaviour. But worse, infinitely worse, since she realized that her beautiful boy was handicapped and, if the specialists were right, then he would remain so for the rest of his life. All she could do was hope against hope that they might have made an error.

As Adam had grown, he had gone through the stages that any other little boy or girl experienced. He had learned to crawl, pulled himself up and toddled, and occasionally would repeat a word or two that he heard. But, as Miriam noticed whenever she saw children of a similar age, Adam's behaviour was always slightly different, subtly out of step.

When she took him to the park, he would remain apart from the other children, apparently unconscious of everything around him except for the two favourite pebbles he would clutch in his hands — one flat, one round — which he would rub together over and over, listening fascinated to the dry, grating sound they made. And if any other child dared to take one of the stones away from him, he would scream and shout in a furious tantrum until the missing object was returned. The other children would soon begin playing with one another — some contest or other with an internal logic of its own, involving running and chasing, touching and wrestling. But Adam would remain unaware of their games and, tightening his fists round the precious pebbles, he would spin round and round and round on the spot without ever becoming dizzy. Finally tiring of this, he would walk away stiffly on tiptoe, his arms and hands flapping.

"Come on then, Adam," Miriam would say when it was time to go home.

But there was never any response. It was as if she didn't exist. He wouldn't come when Miriam called him, he wouldn't listen when she spoke to him, and though his bright blue eyes would gaze around him for hours, it was into empty air, never into her face. If she touched him he would recoil and yet, on the occasions when he wanted something he couldn't reach, he would grab her by the back of the wrist and pull her to do the work for him. She loved the feeling of his little hand on her own, but knew that once the object was in his hand he would ignore her again. He was totally oblivious to the distress he was causing his mother. Cut off, in a world she couldn't reach, Adam remained completely absorbed in his own apparently aimless activities.

All she could do was take one day at a time, expecting nothing but continuing to hope that one day everything would turn out all right.

In many ways, she had learnt to cope with her son's problems better than Derek. He had never been a particularly outgoing man, but since learning of Adam's condition he had retreated still further. For the last eight years he had been working at Dimwell's, a research institute on the outskirts of the town, where cosmetics, toiletries, food additives, tobacco and its substitutes, pesticides and herbicides were all tested to see if they might prove dangerous to humans. Before Adam's birth, he had always been home at six on the dot -- just in time for the news. But, unable to tolerate either the indifference or the screeching of his son, he'd found an increasing number of excuses to stay at work late. Initially, he had phoned Miriam up, but now they both accepted that he never got back much before ten, by which time Adam would usually be tucked up in bed.

Miriam would say that on the day Adam's autism was diagnosed she lost not only the son she thought she had, but also her husband.

Life continued and Adam's fourth birthday came and went. With the experience of the previous year's catastrophic attempt at a party still fresh in her memory, Miriam abandoned the idea of a formal celebration and the pair of them had a big picnic on a blanket in the park. Although unaware of the special significance of the occasion, Adam seemed to enjoy himself. At least he didn't throw a tantrum. It was about two weeks later when something happened that started a chain of events which was to change Adam's life for ever.

"Come on then, Adam," said Miriam. "We're going to see Grandma."

Adam, as usual, took no notice of her whatsoever. He was sitting in the centre of the carpet, his head cocked to one side, his big eyes looking round for something he could hear but not see. It was a posture that Miriam noticed he would adopt increasingly often. At first, she had strained to hear what he was evidently listening to. But it was hopeless. Whatever sounds there were remained silent for her. And at the same time, her own voice went unheard by the little boy.

"Adam!" she repeated, a little more sharply.

Still he continued to swivel his head around slowly, as if tuning in to a distant transmission. Miriam went over to him and crouched down in front of him.

"Adam," she whispered gently, taking hold of his arms and trying to make him look at her.

He struggled for a couple of seconds and threatened to scream.

"We're going to see Grandma. On the bus," she added.

Adam looked at her for an instant.

"Yes," she said. "The bussssssss."

The long hissing sound made him smile momentarily. She wasn't sure why, but from the first time she had taken him for a bus-ride, he had loved the sound of the compressed air being released when the doors were opened and closed. He would smile appreciatively every time it happened and had never resorted to the ear-piercing screech of terror and fury he had maintained on his first and last trip on a train. Buses were good, and from the long 's' that Miriam stressed at the end of the word, he knew that he would soon be hearing those wonderful hissing doors once again.

She helped him get ready. It was quicker in the long run. And by eleven o'clock the two of them were on the number 21, travelling across town to spend the day with her mother; Adam's grandmother. Adam sat on the bench seat, his legs dangling down the side, watching the doors.

"Whoosh-shuk!" he went, in unison with the doors as the air hissed and they opened and closed.

A couple of people looked at the little boy with obvious affection. He looked so sweet. Miriam knew that in a few years this habit, which was endearing in a pre-school youngster, would point him out as a strange child, an abnormal child, a handicapped child. But no. She couldn't let herself think like that. One day at a time: that was her motto. And she smiled back at the other passengers, glad only that Adam was so obviously content.

They were getting near their stop and Miriam was beginning to feel a little bit anxious about how she would get Adam off the bus without any problems. The last time, he had screamed blue murder when she had dared to take him away from the comforting whooshing sound.

Something, however, was different this particular morning, she noticed. Adam had apparently lost interest in the doors and was staring intently at the woman on the back seat who had got on at the stop before.

"Adam," whispered Miriam, trying to draw his attention away from the increasingly agitated woman. "Adam!"

Feeling embarrassed herself, Miriam looked over at the woman and smiled somewhat sheepishly. She was in her fifties, with crisp blue hair and a thick layer of pink face-pack plastered over her wrinkled skin. She was wearing a huge, black fur-coat, which was strange as it was June and the weather wasn't bad at all. Either she felt the cold particularly badly or she wanted to impress people with her wealth. The woman chose to ignore Miriam's smile and looked out of the window.

One of the characteristics of children like Adam is that they find it impossible to tell lies. And not understanding why it should ever be necessary to avoid the truth, her son had often done and said things which had made Miriam wish the ground could swallow her up. Today was to prove no exception. With his concentration now totally diverted from the doors and on to the woman, he suddenly opened his mouth and bellowed.

"Fat!" he yelled. "FAT!!"

And just in case there might be any doubt who he meant, his little hand sprung up and pointed directly at the woman in the fur-coat.

"Adam, shhhh!" said Miriam, pulling him back. But he wriggled out of her grasp, jumped down off the seat and scampered over to the indignant woman.

"FAT!" he shouted again and plunged his head and arms deep into the folds of thick fur. "Fat," he repeated, followed by another word. "Woman" or "warm" — it wasn't clear as his words were muffled by the mouthful of fur.

Horrified, Miriam leapt up from her seat and pulled Adam off the woman, who was by now squealing with

14

shock and horror as the little boy continued to burrow deep into her lap.

"I'm so . . ." Miriam began to say.

But it was pointless. The woman was inconsolable and Miriam decided to get off the bus immediately and walk the rest of the way. With Adam dangling over her arm, she picked up her bag and made her way past the rows of grinning passengers to the doors.

"Whoosh-shuk!" Adam said gleefully as the door closed behind him.

Painfully embarrassing though the whole episode might have been at the time, Miriam found herself dwelling on it for some considerable while afterwards. The woman in the fur-coat had naturally been appalled by the interest the small child had suddenly paid her, but Miriam saw in the incident the first display of real curiosity Adam had ever shown another creature. It occurred to her that he must be lonely. That he needed a playmate. And working on a hunch, she went out and arranged for a companion for her son.

From the moment Oscar entered the house, the change in Adam was evident. Whereas he had never responded to his mother or father, or to the doctors who had tried to carry out IQ tests on him, or to the children in the park, the instant he and Oscar were introduced they hit it off immediately, which was strange — for Oscar was a cat.

—2—
OSCAR CAME TO STAY

When Miriam had placed the basket down on the floor and unbuckled the door, the cat had immediately trotted over towards Adam, who was sitting cross-legged on the carpet, and began rubbing its head against the boy's knees and back.

'Who are you?' Adam thought out loud to his new companion. 'And what are you doing?' he giggled as the cat's soft fur tickled him.

'The name's Oscar,' the cat thought back, 'and I'm scent-setting.'

'What's that?'

'When I rub here,' it thought, nuzzling its head against Adam's elbows, 'and do this,' it added, scratching down the front of his dungarees, 'tiny droplets of scent come out from behind my ears and paws.'

'I can't smell it,' thought Adam, leaning over and sniffing at the bib and braces.

'But I can.'

'And what's it for?'

'It's how we cats claim territory for ourselves,' it explained.

'But I'm not yours,' thought Adam and laughed.

'You are now,' thought Oscar, rubbing its head once more against Adam's knee. 'All mine.'

"Oh, Oscar!" Adam said aloud, hugging the cat towards him and rubbing its head with his cheek.

Miriam had been watching every one of the boy's reactions with increasing fascination. She realized that something very special was happening: that whatever wall Adam had been locked behind was rapidly crumbling away. When he suddenly came out with the cat's name, she was dumbstruck.

She had got Oscar from the RSPCA – if she hadn't taken it, they would probably have put it to sleep. Oscar was one of an abandoned litter which had been found tied up in a sack next to the railway-line the week before. The two boys who had found them had persuaded their parents to keep one each, but the remaining three had been delivered to the dispensary to be looked after or put down. Cats arrived there every day and the staff named them from the walkie-talkie words for the alphabet. Having already reached the letter 'N' that week, the day's intake of eight kittens were accordingly dubbed Oscar, Papa, Quebec, Romeo, Sierra, Tango, Uniform and Victor.

Oscar was undoubtedly the 'character' of the bunch and Miriam was never in any doubt as to which cat she would take home for her son. The man who had pulled it out of the enclosure had said that, of course, she didn't have to keep their name, and that, in fact, Oscar was a 'she' not a 'he'. But Miriam had liked the name and decided to stick with it. The thing was, she was quite positive that since entering the house, she hadn't once mentioned the name.

"How did you know his name was Oscar?" she asked Adam gently.

'Careful!' Oscar instructed. 'I don't think this is the moment to tell her that we can think-speak to each other.'

"Adam?" she repeated.

"You tell," he blurted out without looking up.

Had she, after all? Miriam wondered to herself. She thought back to the words of instruction and advice she had received from the specialist when she had first been told about Adam's condition. Autistic children cannot lie, the doctor had said. They see no reason why they should not tell the truth, and, in any case, they lack the necessary verbal skills to do so. Miriam looked at the little boy happily playing with the cat, Oscar. Either she had been mistaken or, if Adam *had* been telling her a fib, then perhaps the doctors had been wrong all along. It occurred to her that she must be the only mother alive hoping that her son had just lied to her! Time would tell.

Too excited to allow herself so much hope for fear of being disappointed, Miriam went into the kitchen and began busying herself over lunch.

'She's gone,' thought Oscar. 'We can talk. You're Adam, I take it?'

'Adam,' he confirmed.

'And I'm Oscar. Stupid name for a female, but the man at the dispensary wasn't very observant,' she snorted. 'Anyway, Oscar is only my pet name. My *real* name is Mingwaal. It means Protector.'

'Mingwaal,' Adam repeated.

'Yeah,' thought Oscar, 'but your accent is all human. You've got to pronounce it like a cat. Like this.' And the cat yowled her name out loud.

Adam tried to copy her.

'Not bad, I suppose. But I think maybe we'd better stick to Oscar. And how old are you?'

'Old?' thought Adam.

'Your age,' Oscar explained. 'I'm seven months old.'

'I . . . don't know.'

Cats don't live as long as humans. In fact, for every year that a person lives, a cat has aged seven times as much. As Adam was just over four years old and Oscar had been born exactly seven months earlier, by an incredible coincidence, on the day that Oscar was brought to the house, they were both exactly the same age. It would be the one and only time that this would be the case. From that moment on, for every day that passed for Adam, Oscar would age the equivalent of a week.

But that was something that would only become important later on.

'So,' thought Oscar, deciding to abandon any further questions about the boy's age and looking around the room, 'this looks like a nice place. Why don't you show me about a bit.'

Adam followed the cat's gaze. It occurred to him with a sudden shock that he hardly knew where he was. He had remained practically unaware of the house he had been living in since he was born and, as his eyes examined the various corners of the room, he realized that there was scarcely anything he recognized.

Oscar looked at the boy and noticed how bewildered he was becoming.

'Well, perhaps we should go exploring together,' she suggested.

'Come on, then,' said Adam, standing up.

Without any more prompting, Oscar leapt from the carpet and came to land on the settee with a bounce. Without pausing for a second, she sprung up on to the back and then launched herself off into mid-air and flew outstretched to the chair.

"Whee-ow!" Oscar cried as she landed and bounced against the back cushion. 'Come on, Adam. This is fun!' she urged the boy.

Tentatively at first, Adam climbed up on to the settee. He felt all wobbly and unsteady as he tried to stand still.

'JUMP!' Oscar instructed.

And Adam did as he was told. Little nervous hops at first, just to get his balance. But before too long, he was trampolining as high as he possibly could on the springy surface. Up and down and then over, he would leap to the chair and continue bouncing and then, whoosh, off again to the other chair. Higher and higher and then, summoning all his courage, he flew up into the air and dived over to the settee, landed flat on his stomach and burst out laughing.

'And you mean you've never done this before?' Oscar asked.

'Never,' said Adam, lying on the settee, hot and panting. He hadn't even noticed the bits of furniture before.

'Oh well, better late than never,' Oscar thought. 'Come on, let's have another go.'

And they continued bouncing round the room from chair to chair to flying leap and down on to the settee.

Miriam stood in the doorway watching them. If she hadn't just accidentally burnt her arm painfully on the grill, she would have pinched herself to make sure she wasn't dreaming. Yesterday, and the day before, and the day before that, for as far back as she could remember, her son had always been sitting motionless on the floor when she had come to fetch him for lunch. With his eyes staring into space, his ears listening to those sounds she couldn't make out, he would remain unconscious of her presence. And when she spoke to him, he would ignore her.

Today, he was leaping around the furniture like any other four-year-old.

Suddenly catching sight of the person watching him, Adam let himself fall down on to the chair. He sat there, legs sticking out, head bowed with a big silly grin on his face. Oscar leapt up on to his lap and began purring as loud as a motor bike.

"Well, what have you two been up to?" asked Miriam.

"Fun," said Adam simply.

"Fun, eh?" she repeated. "Then you must be pretty hungry by now. Come on."

Adam remained seated on the chair.

'Come on, idiot,' Oscar insisted, leaping off Adam's legs. 'It's lunch-time.'

Miriam was beginning to believe in miracles. For the first time ever, Adam responded properly to her. Climbing down off the chair, he toddled into the kitchen on his own without needing either to be carried screaming, or left for her to bring the meal to him.

It couldn't all be this easy, Miriam thought to herself. Could it? How could the arrival of a stray moggy cause such a sudden reversal in his behaviour. It made no sense. No sense at all.

But she didn't care how illogical it might be. All she knew was that something unbelievably magical was taking place. And as Oscar lapped at her milk and Adam inexpertly dipped his Marmite soldiers into the soft-boiled eggs and slurped at his orange juice, neither of them noticed the tears welling up in Mrs Miriam Williams' eyes. Tears, not of the usual despair she felt, but of relief and inexpressible happiness.

It began raining heavily after lunch and as Oscar hated getting wet, she suggested examining the rest of the house. There was so much to see. For Adam, who had spent the whole of his short life so far in a kind of dream-world, unable to make sense of the constant bombardment of sounds and visions he had been confronted with, the investigation was like a journey of discovery. He had scarcely been able to understand anything his mum or dad had said to him. The sounds that came from their mouths had refused to form themselves into anything of meaning. But with Oscar, all that had suddenly changed. The fog had lifted. The radio had been tuned. And it brought with it the relief an interpreter brings to a traveller in a strange land, alone and unable to understand a single word of the language spoken there.

'And what's this?' Oscar asked, knocking a large wooden toy with her paw.

Adam shrugged. His bedroom was full of pictures and objects he couldn't remember ever having seen before in his life.

'It's some kind of a boat,' thought Oscar.

'A boat?'

'For travelling on water,' Oscar explained. 'Undo that clasp there — paws and claws have a lot of uses, but they're not much good at opening doors.'

Adam did as he was told.

'Now what's inside?'

'These,' thought Adam, pulling out a handful of tiny wooden objects, which he laid down on the floor next to the boat.

'Animals,' said Oscar. 'Let's see: elephants, giraffes, zebras, lions and tigers — they're related to me, you know,' she added proudly. 'Rhinos, hippos, chimps, snakes . . . Yes, they all seem to be here.'

Adam looked intently at the models. He had never heard of Noah's Ark, but as he fingered the collection of striped and spotted, horned and tusked, long, short and tall animals, a feeling stirred inside him. For the first time, he felt that there was something familiar about what he could see. And

22

as he closed his eyes, there again was that distant confusion of sounds that he had been able to hear since he was born. One by one, he picked up the different animals and looked at them in turn. He twisted his head round slightly as he did so. The sounds he could hear changed slightly each time. Just what *was* out there?

Hours passed as Adam played with the Ark: pairing the animals off, marching them up the gangplank, listening carefully to what they might be saying to him. However closely he listened though, he was unable to make out a single word. Soon tiring of the Ark, Oscar had jumped up on to the end of the bed, curled up and fallen asleep. Miriam had poked her head around the door a couple of times, but had decided to leave Adam playing. She wanted to join in his game, but so much had happened that day already that she felt she ought to leave well alone for the time being. At his bed-time, though, she came in.

"Adam," she said softly.

The little boy continued moving the animals around on deck, apparently deaf to her voice. Miriam felt a tremor of panic running up and down her spine. Surely she hadn't imagined the whole mysterious change.

"Adam," she said, a little louder.

Still he remained unaware that she was standing there. Oscar rolled over on the bed, stretched her legs out and yawned widely. She opened her eyes and saw the little boy sitting on the floor in exactly the same position as when she had left him. Mrs Williams, the kind lady who had rescued her from the dispensary, was leaning over her son looking worried.

'Adam!' Oscar snapped.

The boy spun round.

'What?'

'Your mother,' she hissed.

'I didn't notice,' he thought back, and looked up into his mother's anxious face and smiled.

Miriam smiled back. "Beddy-byes," she said.

Adam held his arms up in the air to be hoisted up. Miriam stared down incredulously for a second. He had never done that before. A moment later, and she had swept him up off the floor and lugged him happily into the bathroom for his teeth and toilet routine. Oscar padded in after them, and as Adam's mother wet the face-cloth and put toothpaste on his toothbrush, the cat instructed him how to move his body around so that he wouldn't be the awkward lump he usually was when his mother was getting him ready for bed.

Having tucked him in, Miriam sat on the bed and stroked Adam's temples.

"Welcome back," she whispered. "I don't know where you've been all these years, but I'm so, so glad you've decided to come back to me. And you," she said, tickling Oscar under the chin, "heaven knows what you've done, but thank you. If only I'd come across you four years ago."

Oscar purred appreciatively.

"Good grief," she said to herself suddenly. "If Derek could hear me like this, chatting away to a cat, he'd make me go and see a psychiatrist."

As she switched the light off, she turned round and looked back from the doorway. Adam on his side under the duvet, Oscar curled up by his arm.

"Night-night," she said. "Sleep well. Both of you."

Adam remained silent.

'Oy!' Oscar thought out loud. 'Say "night-night, Mummy",' she instructed.

"Night-night, Mummy," said Adam sleepily.

"Pleasant dreams, darling," she replied, almost beside

herself with happiness to have had a response from her little boy. She slid the door to.

Adam was woken some time later by the sound of angry voices. It was night-time still, but an almost full moon was up and the room was bathed in a silvery light. He looked over to where Oscar was lying. Her head was lifted high and the moonlight was reflected brightly in her eyes.

'What's happening?' asked Adam.

Oscar laid her head down on her folded paws.

'Let's just say I prefer your mum,' Oscar thought back.

Adam tried his best to listen to the raised and slightly muffled words of his mother and father, but he was too unused to tuning in to the sound of human voices, and apart from the odd phrase or two, none of it made a great deal of sense. And yet certain words — the words that his father shouted out the loudest — fixed themselves in his memory.

A simpleton.

A congenital idiot.

He was born a half-wit, he remains a half-wit!

Unpleasant words that Adam knew were being used unkindly. He asked Oscar what they all meant, but the cat's eyes were closed and she refused to reply.

'I feel frightened,' the little boy thought.

Oscar, only feigning sleep all along, moved up the bed a little and began purring.

'Leave it till the morning,' she said. 'Just listen to me and go back to sleep.'

And that was what Adam did. He lay his head back down and concentrated on the sound of Oscar's throaty purr. It was deep and comforting, and as he drifted off again, the angry words from the next room were shut out and his head began to fill with the distant sounds he knew so well.

The following morning it was Oscar who woke up first. Having prowled around the room, leapt up on to the window-ledge and ascertained that it was a sunny day outside, she decided that it was about time Adam woke up too. She jumped back on the bed and licked at Adam's face, purring as loudly as a revving lorry.

'Oscar!' he thought out loud happily as he opened his eyes and found himself looking straight into the furry face of his new playmate.

'About time too,' the cat replied gruffly, and cuffed Adam across the nose with her padded paw.

'OK, OK,' said Adam, swinging his legs off the bed and jumping down to the floor.

'Right,' Oscar thought, 'so are you going to get dressed?'

'On my own?'

'Well, I can't help you — except to tell you what to do,' the cat thought back to him. 'And you *are* over four years old now.'

'All right then,' said Adam.

'Right, first of all, you've got to take off your pyjamas.'

Adam did as he was instructed. He found the buttons on his pyjama-top the most fiddly, but when they were all undone, the rest was a piece of cake. He pulled up his pants, tucked in his T-shirt and wriggled into his dungarees. Shoelaces would have defeated him totally, but luckily his plimsolls were elasticated.

'Well done,' Oscar thought. 'Have a look at yourself and brush your hair.'

'Have a look at yourself,' Adam repeated.

'Not *my*self, *your*self,' the cat explained and trotted over to the full-length mirror by the door. 'What a superbly athletic example of my species I am,' she said, parading back and forwards in front of her reflection. 'Look at the poise, the agility, the fur – you'd save yourself a lot of time in the morning if you had a nice fur-coat like me.'

'It would get all dirty,' thought Adam.

'You have to look after it, of course,' Oscar agreed, twisting her head round and licking clean a matted patch of fur she had spotted at the base of her tail. 'We haven't all got washing-machines,' she added sniffily.

'That's me,' Adam thought, staring at himself in the mirror.

'Of course it is,' the cat replied. 'Who did you expect to see? Puss in Boots?'

'I never ...' Adam started. He kept looking at himself, noting everything about the way he looked. The big blue eyes and straight fair fringe, the small nose and ears that stuck out a little. They were all his. He wanted to make sure he remembered everything so that he would recognize himself the next time.

'Hair,' Oscar instructed.

'Oh yes,' said Adam and, watching the reflection of his hands in the mirror, he groped around on the table for the brush. Then, using both hands and all the concentration he could muster, he pulled it across his head, dragging the hair to one side. It felt nice.

Everything was that little bit special that morning, with him getting ready by himself. Well, almost by himself.

'Let's go, Oscar,' he thought, laying the brush down.

'Words I never thought I'd hear,' the cat replied, trotting towards the door with her tail held high.

From the top of the stairs, Adam could hear his parents talking at the breakfast table. This, he knew, was unusual. Most mornings when he got up it would just be him and his mum.

'It's Saturday,' Oscar explained. 'No work today.'

'Saturday,' Adam repeated as he started off down the stairs. He'd never liked stairs. They always looked such a horribly long way down from the top. But watching Oscar's swishing tail rather than the hall floor below him, Adam found that if he held tightly on to the banisters and took it one step at a time, there was absolutely no problem.

He followed Oscar into the kitchen.

His mum and dad were sitting at the table eating toast, drinking coffee and flipping through their newspapers. Adam looked at them carefully. He realized that he'd never really even looked at *them* before. They didn't look like one another at all, and fresh from the mirror, he recognized that it was his mother he took after. She, like him, was blonde with clear, caramelly skin. His father, on the other hand, had dark hair, thinning across the top. His eyes were dark and his sunken cheeks and bony jaw were covered with a dark shadow of stubble. Unlike his wife, who was tall and athletic, Derek Williams was thin and short. With tight lips and, as Adam had always unconsciously recognized, a meanly short temper.

Oscar miaowed loudly to announce their presence.

"The cat, I presume," said Derek.

"Her name's Oscar," said Miriam, looking round.

At that moment they both noticed their little boy. Simultaneously, they leapt to their feet and stared down at him, mouths open. It was Derek who spoke first.

"You did undress him last night, I take it."

Miriam burst out crying, swung Adam off the floor and held him tightly to herself. She kissed him over and over on his forehead.

"You see, you see," she sobbed to her husband. "I *told* you."

Derek moved round behind his wife's shoulder and looked at Adam.

"He's even tried to brush his hair," he said, intrigued despite himself.

"He's wonderful," said Miriam, wiping her tears away on the back of her hand.

It was all going a bit fast for Adam, but he recognized the words 'brush' and 'hair'. He smiled and reached up to touch it again.

"Oscar telled," he explained. "Oscar telled."

"Oscar!" said Derek sarcastically.

'I warned you,' Oscar thought as sharply as she could to the boy.

"The cat?" Derek asked.

Adam nodded dumbly.

"There's me, graduated from Oxford, I've got a doctorate in Applied Biology from Cambridge, but does my son learn anything from his father? Does he heck? And who does he learn from? From a cat."

"Be quiet," said Miriam, as Adam began to wriggle about fretfully, "you're disturbing him again."

"He already *is* disturbed," said Derek meanly.

And the words that Adam had heard through the wall the night before were repeated. This time, however, they were neither muffled nor unclear.

"The boy is an idiot!"

"Derek!" Miriam shouted.

"He was born a half-wit, he . . ."

"SHUT UP!" Miriam screamed at him.

"If this is your idea of a joke . . ." he yelled. "Oh, to hell with it. I'm going to work. I get more sense out of the laboratory animals."

And with that, he strode across the kitchen, kicking at the cat as he did so, and slammed the front door behind him.

Miriam placed Adam gently back on the floor. Oscar trotted over and rubbed against his leg affectionately.

'Ignore him,' Oscar thought dismissively. 'If there was an idiot in the kitchen a moment ago, it certainly wasn't you.'

Adam smiled.

"There's a good boy," said Miriam, relieved that he hadn't taken it too badly. "Daddy didn't mean it. He's just . . . Why don't you and Oscar go and play in the garden while I get breakfast ready?"

—3—
A VERY SPECIAL SCHOOL

'But what if I just say no,' Adam persisted.

'You can't,' Oscar thought back. 'They wouldn't allow you to, and, anyway, it would be stupid to refuse. You *need* to go.'

Adam looked at the cat long and hard.

'Oscar, I'm frightened.'

The reason for Adam's unease was that having reached the ripe old age of five, the question of school had arisen. The progress that Miriam had seen in her son had been so remarkable that she had hoped he might be taken at the local primary school. But there had been problems. All his medical notes testified to the fact that as a baby, Adam Williams had been diagnosed 'autistic'. Of course, she had insisted that new tests be carried out. *She* lived with him. *She* knew what he was capable of. Finally, the authorities relented, but the results of the test proved disappointing.

"Obviously there has been an improvement. A very marked improvement," the education officer added encouragingly, "but we nevertheless still feel that it would not be in the boy's best interest to go to the local school."

Miriam wanted to tell them that if only they had let him bring his pet cat along to the test in the first place, the results would have been totally different. But she couldn't, could she? They would think she was crazy. Nobody would believe the changes that had taken place within her son since Oscar's arrival.

"For Adam's *special* condition," the education officer continued tactfully, "he needs a *Special* School."

Miriam looked down at her hands.

"A school with adequate and appropriate equipment, and staff qualified to take care of children with various handicaps.'

"He's *not* handicapped," said Miriam vehemently. "He's not."

"I'm sorry, Mrs Williams. You're right. I used the word ill-advisedly. Let us say 'specialist needs'. Adam, like so many other little children, has needs above and beyond the capabilities of an ordinary school, and St Jude's is better equipped to fulfil those needs than any other school in the area."

Miriam knew that she was beaten.

"It is for Adam's own good," the education officer persisted. "Trust me."

"And if the school turns out to be obviously wrong for him . . .?"

"There is a term-by-term reassessment," she was assured. "You really have absolutely nothing to worry about, Mrs Williams."

To be honest, Miriam had never been in any doubt as to what the outcome of the tests would be. And she recognized the sense in what the education officer had told her. It *would* be better if he were at a school where the staff had been specially trained to look after children with learning difficulties. Despite the advances Adam had made, she would be the first to admit that those difficulties remained. Her biggest fear was the reaction of her husband when she broke the news to him.

Having been initially totally against even keeping the cat in the house, he'd grudgingly had to admit that, for whatever reason, Adam did seem to respond to Oscar's presence. Putting aside his aversion to having any animals at home – after all, he had to work with them at the research institute every day – he allowed the cat to stay. But having made such an uncharacteristic concession, he seemed to expect miracles to take place.

"My son is cured," he would say. "He'll be starting school in a couple of months."

And as the time drew nearer, he would carry out tests of his own on the little boy. Adam, however, still had enormous problems with speaking and listening. There was something about trying to concentrate on human words for any length of time that baffled him and left him feeling totally drained. He could sense his father's impatience, and though he tried his best to answer the way he should, he knew from the clipped replies and pursed lips that he had somehow failed again.

So many of the words sounded similar. And yet his dad would get increasingly exasperated if he said '*in*', instead of '*on* the table'. Pairs of words were a problem as well. Egg and bacon, sock and shoe, dog and cat, black and white – he always knew what he meant when he spoke but by the pale, taut expression that would come over the face in front of him, Adam would know that he had got them confused again.

"Oscar play garden," he would say. Or "Mummy go car shops." However much effort he put into the sentence, the response from his father was always the same cold, humourless irritation. And when Oscar wasn't around, it was even worse.

A couple of months previously, just after Oscar's accident when she had come crashing through the greenhouse roof and dislocated both front legs, Adam and his mum and dad had all been sitting at the table having Sunday dinner. Chicken. Oscar was lying bandaged up in her basket in the kitchen – even the smell of the roast bird couldn't rouse any interest in her. When he had finished eating and wiped his mouth with his napkin, Adam asked the question he had learnt by heart in his best voice. He knew it was what he was meant to say after a meal.

"Can I get down, please?"

"Course you can," his mum had said.

"And what are you going to do when you've got down?" his dad had asked him.

Adam had thought for a moment.

"Stand on floor," he said.

Miriam had laughed at how literally Adam had interpreted the question and hugged him. But Derek had been furious. He slammed his own knife and fork down and strode out of the room, muttering his usual litany of abuse: "Simpleton, idiot, half-wit!"

It wasn't that he intended to be deliberately cruel, but he simply couldn't bear the constant reminders that his son was 'not quite right'. Derek was a scientist: trained to be logical, rational, objective. And here he was with a son who had apparently learned to communicate with the help of his pet cat. It made no sense. And now, every time that Adam did something or said something wrong, Derek felt that he himself had failed in some way.

34

Adam seldom understood the reasons for his father's outbursts. He looked up at his mum.

"Angry," he said.

"Angry," Miriam agreed. "But never mind."

Yes, angry. He was always angry about something or other, and she knew that he would take the news about St Jude's particularly badly. While Adam was at home, Derek could convince himself that his problem was merely temporary, but being sent to a Special School was, in his eyes, giving his son an official seal of condemnation. In the end, she had taken the bull by the horns and spelled it out to him one evening when he had come in late from work.

"Right, fine," was his only response.

"It'll be better for him in the long run," Miriam persisted. "They've got the equipment, the qualified . . ."

"I said 'fine'," he repeated. "I don't want to know anything else about it. Do you understand?" he added, and went to his study. Miriam stood there alone, irritated, but somewhat relieved by her husband's inability to cope with the situation.

One down, one to go, she thought.

The following day, she had tried her best to explain to Adam what the autumn held in store for him. Of course, as he had no idea what a school was anyway, the fact of its being 'special' was neither here nor there. What he did understand from her explanation was that he would have to remain separated from Oscar for countless hours every day.

"Noooooooooooo!" he wailed. "NOOOOOOOOOOO!"

Hearing the agonizing screams, Oscar came bounding back from the next-door pond she had been lying next to, lulling the stupid goldfish into a false sense of security before scooping them out as a light snack. She leapt down from the fence and trotted over to Adam's side.

'What is it?' she asked.

'I've got to go away,' Adam thought back.

"It's only for the mornings at first, Adam," Miriam said, wiping his eyes dry.

'Go where?' Oscar asked.

'Stool.'

'Stool?'

'Something like that. Stool or spool or . . .'

'School!' the cat exclaimed as the word suddenly clicked. 'Ah yes, I'd forgotten you had that to look forward to.'

'Look forward to?' Adam repeated. 'But I don't want to go.'

'Of course you do,' the cat insisted.

'Do I?' Adam asked uncertainly. 'Are you sure?'

'Sure I'm sure.'

Miriam looked at her son carefully. As usual, the presence of the cat had been sufficient to calm him down. Adam was softly stroking Oscar around her ears, and as he did so, he would occasionally smile or frown or nod his head. Apart from the fact that their lips weren't moving, it looked for all the world as though the two of them were deep in conversation. Even if it was all in Adam's imagination, it was clearly real to him. Seeing, sadly, that whatever was being communicated between boy and cat was having a far more comforting effect than she had ever had, Miriam decided to leave the two of them at it.

'But what is a school?' Adam continued.

'It's where loads of boys and girls go to learn about . . . well, everything.'

'But I don't like boys and girls, do I?' Adam thought back miserably.

The trips to the park were still all too familiar. He had never known what the other children were doing. They would run around the whole time, never keeping still, playing strange games that meant nothing to him. Tag

36

games, war games, mime games. And they were always so noisy. Shouting, calling out, whooping like Red Indians, stuttering like machine-guns – strange sounds that Adam couldn't make any sense of.

If that was what school was, there seemed little point in going. He'd learnt more from Oscar than he could ever have learnt from other children. How to climb trees. How to catch mice. And just about all there was to know about babies as he'd watched her grow and grow and finally give birth to the four tiny, blind kittens they'd called Eeny, Meeny, Miney and Mo.

'It just seems stupid,' Adam concluded sullenly.

Oscar had listened to Adam's excuses, explanations and objections without interrupting. She knew how important she'd been to the little boy, but she also recognized her own limitations as far as preparing him for the future.

'The thing is,' she thought to him when he'd finished his little tirade, 'you, Adam, are not a cat.'

'I know that, stupid,' he answered.

'Yes, but do you realize what it means?' Oscar persisted. 'You are a five-year-old boy now. Lots of five-year-olds have playmates – animals, teddies, imaginary friends – but you've got to get ready for being older. And that means being able to talk to people.'

Adam felt shudders of unease at the nape of his neck. He remembered the meaningless jumble of sounds that had swum round and round his head until the day Oscar had come along and made them all clear.

'Apart from anything else,' Oscar continued, 'by the time you leave school when you're sixteen or so, I'll be an old, old lady of eighty-seven – if I'm still alive at all. You won't be able to rely on me any more then, Adam.'

A painful lump came into the little boy's throat.

'You're not ... dying, are you?' he asked, remembering

37

the lifeless lumps of fur they had found down by the stream where the rat poison had been put down.

'Not for a long time,' Oscar reassured him. 'But certainly before you.'

He wanted to say something, but even think-talking, the words weren't there. All he could sense was an echoing, bottomless sadness.

"Love you, Oscar," Adam said in real words and hugged her tightly.

'Hey, hey,' the cat protested. 'I'm not going to last five minutes if you go squeezing me like that.'

Adam giggled and let her go.

'So you think I'll be OK, do you?'

'You're going to be fine.'

'I wish you could come with me, though,' Adam thought. 'It's all so complicated when you're not around.'

'It won't be,' Oscar said.

'How can you be so certain?'

'Cos you're going to a *very special* school,' the cat informed him. 'I heard them talking about it.'

'Special? How?'

'All the children there are like you,' said Oscar. 'Not like the kids in the park, so you needn't worry. You *will* understand them and you'll make so many friends you just won't believe it.'

'Honest?'

'Honest.'

'You really promise?'

'Adam, I promise. And if I'm wrong ...' Oscar looked around briefly. 'You can cut off my tail.'

—4—
MISSING

In the event, Adam hadn't had to transform Oscar into a Manx cat, and three years later she would still stalk around the house and garden with her tail held high. Everything Oscar had said to Adam had come true. He *had* found the other children easier to understand. He *had* made lots of friends. And, with the patient help of the friendly teachers there, he had learnt more than he would have thought possible. Oscar had been right – although she had helped him so much, there were areas where her knowledge simply didn't extend. As she had said: she wasn't a human and Adam wasn't a cat.

It had taken him a long time, but gradually over the three years since he had started at St Jude's, Adam had learnt to write. Unlike most children, once he got the hang of it, he found it a much easier thing to do than speak. All the thoughts were there in his head anyway, and with writing he could take his time, making sure that every single word was correct before putting it down.

"That's very good," Derek would say when Adam showed him some of his homework, and the boy would beam proudly.

Derek had to admit that Adam had improved a great deal at St Jude's, and though he still felt curiously guilty about the difficulties his son had in communicating, he was beginning to feel a bit more optimistic about the future. On the page, his son was equal to any other kid his age, and Derek revived his hopes that, one day, Adam too might become a scientist.

Speaking, however, was still a problem. It was all so fast and never seemed to come automatically. Adam would still get totally unrelated words confused: candlestick for mushroom; flannel for bottle; kettle for piano. And when he tried to make a sentence, the word order would sometimes still come out all wrong: "Bus school late coming." But it certainly wasn't that he didn't know the rules. His writing proved that. And when he wrote, all the little problems were ironed away completely.

St Jude's believed in as much parent involvement as possible, and frequent evening exhibitions were held so that the children's progress could be monitored. On her last visit to the school, Miriam had been looking at a selection of the children's work which was pinned to the wall, when she had come to a poem decorated with a drawing of a large tabby cat.

First Day

I can still remember
The first day
When the bus came
And took me away

To the world outside
Of distant voices
A jumbled mess
Of ugly noises

And bit by bit
I understood
Just like Oscar
Said I would

Adam Williams, aged 8

"Are you all right?" one of the teachers had asked Miriam, seeing her standing in the corner of the hall with tears streaming down her cheeks.

"Fine, fine," Miriam had said. "I just . . . I don't know. I never thought he'd ever write anything so . . ." she sobbed out loud again.

"It's young Adam, isn't it?" the teacher said. "A remarkable little boy – we're all very proud of the progress he's made."

"He *is* getting better, isn't he?" she asked weakly, scarcely daring to hear the answer.

"Mrs Williams, this poem would not be out of place in any primary school in the country," the teacher confirmed. "It's a remarkably sensitive piece of work. Is Oscar his father?"

Miriam laughed, bitterly. Even though Derek was a little better with the boy now, she still found it difficult to forgive all his outbursts. Even if Derek hadn't been responsible for Adam's condition, he certainly hadn't helped the boy improve.

"No," she said. "*She's* a cat. Adam's cat – he's had her since she was a kitten."

It was the teacher's turn to laugh.

"That would explain it then," she said.

41

"Explain what?"

"Adam's remarkable aptitude for gymnastics. I've never seen a more graceful child. His body is so supple, and on the bars and ropes he can climb and balance, well . . ." she laughed again, "like a cat."

"He *has* become more agile," Miriam agreed. "He used to be so stiff."

"We're having a gymnastics evening in a month's time," the teacher continued, "you *must* come along. I think you're going to be very surprised."

It wasn't only in poetry and gymnastics that Adam had shone. It hadn't been long after his arrival that the teachers had noticed his remarkable sense of rhythm.

Although he had never played with his two pebbles after Oscar arrived, Adam hadn't thrown them away. Instead, he'd stored them in the hold of the Ark alongside the wooden animals: the round one balanced on the flat one. Realizing that he would have to travel to that first day at school without Oscar, he'd slipped the two comforting stones into his pocket just before the bus arrived to whisk him off. Throughout the journey, he had rubbed them together quietly, listening to the soft, dry scraping noise which made him feel that little bit better.

Without even trying to introduce him to the other children, the teachers had taught the class a simple song. At first Adam hadn't wanted to join in, and when he was given a triangle to play, he had thrown it angrily at the wall. But as the music had got under way, he found that the beat got right inside him. He couldn't keep still. And finding himself now without a percussion instrument to hit, he took out the two familiar pebbles and began tapping them together in increasingly complicated rhythms.

This was the start.

Over the years, he learnt to use all the percussion

instruments they had in the music room: tambourines and tom-toms, kettledrums, castanets and maracas. And when he discovered the glockenspiel, it heralded the switch from rhythm to melody. Something within the shifting notes of the music reminded Adam of the distant sounds he'd heard as a baby – the sounds he still heard when he was lying in bed at night.

There was another boy at the school who was, as the teachers called it, 'gifted' in music. His name was Errol, and though he had even more problems than Adam in talking, the two of them managed just fine.

"Listen," said Errol, as he placed his fingers down on the piano and began playing a weird tune. Some of the combinations of notes sounded discordant at first, some of the chords seemed to clash, and yet as Adam listened and watched Errol's face, he understood. In the same way that Adam could communicate with Oscar in a way that no one understood, so Errol communicated through music.

And lots of the other kids at St Jude's were the same. There are so many doors to communication. Bees perform a special dance in the hive to inform the others of the whereabouts of nectar-filled flowers; impalas release a scent from their heels which alerts the rest of the herd to danger as they leap away from an approaching cheetah, while whales sing continuously of the changing history of the entire ocean. And while it is undoubtedly true that the vast majority of new-born babies tune in to their parents' voices and learn from them, it is also the case that many children take a quite different route to communication. For some, like Adam and Errol, it is merely a detour. For others, like Elaine, who would stare for hours at the chattering clouds that only she could hear, and Oliver, who would swirl and stir paint around with his fingers, making multi-coloured patterns like oil on water, their journeys would take much longer.

They were *all*, as Oscar had said, SPECIAL.

Adam was happy. He looked forward to going to school every day, to being with the other children. Yet by late afternoon, when it was time for the bus to take them all back home he was already looking forward to seeing Oscar again. And his mum. Time continued to pass at St Jude's and without really noticing, Adam found that the longer he stayed in these relaxed surroundings, the easier it was becoming to talk. And not only by think-speaking to the cat. No, slowly but surely he was learning to speak to ordinary people using real words.

It was the beginning of November and Adam's class were all coming to the end of a project on Guy Fawkes Night. Everyone had done something. Oliver had taken control of the painting and had covered huge pieces of paper with the most brilliant display of exploding and cascading fireworks ever. You could almost hear the excited 'ooohs' and 'aaahs' just looking at them. The paintings were being pinned up all round the walls and over the ceiling. Adam and several of the others, dressed up in rocket and Catherine wheel costumes they had made, had transformed themselves into fireworks. They were practising a gymnastics routine of flick-flacks, cartwheels and somersaults, with Errol and Alison supplying the music.

Their display was going to be a million times more fantastic than the official council spectacular in the park. Adam couldn't wait to get back to tell Oscar all about it. She didn't like the loud bangs of real fireworks and would appreciate the idea of the children putting on their own pretend display.

"Oscar!" he called, leaping down from the school-bus outside his house.

"Hello, darling," his mum said, as he pushed open the front door.

"Hi," he said.

"How was school?"

"Brill," he said. "Doing fireworks for a special display."

"What, real ones?"

"No. Realer than real," he said. "We the fireworks! Where's Oscar?"

It occurred to Miriam that she hadn't seen Oscar around all day. Normally, the cat would be performing figure eights around her ankles at this time in the afternoon, waiting to be fed. She opened the kitchen window and called her.

There was the sound of a couple of premature bangers, but no sign of the cat.

"She'll be around somewhere," said his mum. "Go and get yourself washed up for tea."

Adam went up to the bathroom and turned on the taps to wash his hands and face. But as he stood there, his mind began to wander and he heard the familiar distant voices. Despite all the time he had spent with Oscar, and despite all he had learnt at school, Adam was still confused about the peculiar sounds that filled his head. He had no idea either where they came from or what they were. But as he listened even closer, he thought he could hear the distant, whimpering voice of Oscar pleading for help. Adam tilted his head to the side to try to hear more clearly. But the sound was gone again. In its place, he became conscious of angry words coming from much closer to home.

"For heaven's sake, Adam," Miriam was saying. "Watch what you're doing."

Looking down, Adam saw the water gushing out of the taps he'd forgotten to turn off and cascading over the side of the bowl. He was already standing in a warm pool which was spreading out over the lino. Miriam rushed over, pulled the plug out and stopped the flow of water.

"Now, what's the matter?" she asked, crouching down to mop up the pool with the bathmat.

"Oscar," said Adam. "I'm worried. Always here, except now."

Miriam had to concede that what her son was saying was true. In the three years since Adam had first started going to school, Oscar had always been there, ready to greet the little boy on his return. Why should today be any different?

"Maybe she's got a new boyfriend," said Miriam.

"Makes no difference," Adam replied sullenly.

"Look," said Miriam, "come down and have something to eat and then we'll go out looking for her. All right?"

Adam had never eaten his dinner more quickly before. Fish fingers, chips, peas, tomatoes and chocolate blancmange all disappeared from sight in the time it took Miriam to boil the kettle for a cup of tea. At first she refused to believe that he could have eaten it at all.

"Come on," she said, "where have you put it?"

"Gone."

"I can see it's gone, but where?"

Adam pointed down his throat theatrically and grinned. The debris from his meal, which was splattered down his T-shirt, seemed to confirm the story.

"Can we go out now?" he asked.

Miriam sighed. "All right," she said. "But put your anorak on. It's cold out."

They walked around for over an hour. Adam was becoming increasingly agitated, and as he called out the missing cat's name, his voice gradually rose to an anguished screech as his fears for Oscar's safety grew. Miriam too felt herself tensing up. She hadn't seen her son so upset for years, and the thought of his returning to the uncontrolled, hysterical tantrums of his toddling days began to haunt her. The

46

longer they searched, the more his tenuous grasp on the language began to falter.

"Where Oscar, where Oscar, where Oscar?" he repeated over and over.

Although it was still the day before Guy Fawkes Night, bangers and crackers were already exploding every minute. It was making Miriam jumpy; she knew that the poor cat would be absolutely terrified.

"Oscar hate bangs," said Adam. "Stop bangs, Mummy."

"I know, darling," said Miriam, squeezing his clammy hand tightly.

"Stop bangs," he repeated. "Stop it. Stop it! STOP!! STOP!!!"

The word turned to a frantic scream as Adam's panic reached breaking-point.

"Come on," said Miriam, picking him up and hugging him, "we're going home now. I know what's happened. Oscar has found a nice, safe, quiet place to hide while all the nasty fireworks are going off and she'll be back when it's all over. Now what I want you to do," she continued, trying to keep the boy's mind occupied, "is think nice thoughts to Oscar."

She felt Adam stop wriggling.

"That's it. Nice, nice thoughts. Like Oscar gives you when you're upset. Well, she's probably all frightened at the moment, because of the loud bangs, so you let her know that there's no need to worry and tell her to stay where she is until it's safe to come out again."

"Nice thoughts," Adam repeated.

"The nicest thoughts in the world," said Miriam.

That evening, Adam played with his Ark. Taking all the animals out and lining them up on the carpet, he gave them a good talking to.

'And I want you to let her know that she's all right,' he

thought. 'Especially you,' he added, picking up the lion and lioness, 'and you and you and you,' he added to the tigers, leopards and cheetahs. 'She said you were all in the same family, so just do what an auntie or an uncle would do and tell her not to worry.'

It took Adam an unusually long time to fall asleep. Normally, he would get into bed, and with the sound of Oscar purring in his ear, he would drop off in an instant. This evening was different. He tossed and turned for what seemed like hours, unable to keep at bay those disturbing, distant sounds of howling, barking, roaring. Some time long after his mum had turned off the television and gone to bed, he heard the key in the lock as his dad arrived home.

"I haven't got a clue where the cat is," he heard him saying from the bedroom.

"Are you sure? I'd still like to know how you managed to find homes for all those kittens. If I even *thought* she might have ended up at Dimwell's . . ."

"You're talking rubbish," he interrupted. "I haven't seen it. I don't know where it is. I don't *care* where it is!"

"Well, you should do. I haven't seen him so upset for years."

"And what am I supposed to do about it?"

Adam pulled the pillow over his head. Their arguments never made much sense anyway. Why should his father want to take Oscar to work with him?

'Nice thoughts' he remembered his mother saying, and those were what he sent to Oscar, who was out there somewhere in the cold, dark night. Fish and mice and cream and warm sun and soft bed and tickles behind the ear and all the other thoughts that Adam knew would make her feel good. Wherever she was.

The indoor fireworks show the children put on was indeed

spectacular — but Adam's heart wasn't in it. The black mural all around the room created the perfect atmosphere, and where the light from the windows shone through the layers of coloured tissue paper it looked like real exploding rockets. Errol and Alison's music, with its drum rolls and cymbal crashes, was the perfect accompaniment to the display, and in their costumes, Adam and the other fireworks ran, spun, dipped and dived around the classroom in the most energetic performance anyone had ever put on. The finale, introduced by a rhythmical pounding of all the bass drums which grew louder and louder until every single instrument was being struck simultaneously, involved all the children standing round the room whirling sparklers this way and that in a thousand different patterns.

As the last flashing stick of white fire fizzled out, someone put the lights on and all the teachers who had come to watch the display burst into applause.

"Bravo!" they called.

For Adam, the best part of the whole afternoon was the fact that they could go home early. The school had decided that as there was a council fireworks display on in the early evening, they would allow the children to leave at three o'clock so that they could have some tea before the official opening. Adam was the first one at the school gates waiting for the arrival of the bus.

"Are you OK, Adam?" he heard someone asking him.

He turned round. It was Mr Grant. He nodded, silently.

"Cat got your tongue?" he asked, inadvertently using the most inappropriate turn of phrase he could have managed and making Adam melt into tears.

"Oscar's gone," he bawled out.

"And who's Oscar?"

"My cat!" he howled even louder.

The teacher made all the appropriate noises and

assurances that the cat would turn up, but Adam was by this time sobbing uncontrollably. He was still sniffling when he got out of the bus outside his house. All the way back, he'd been repeating over and over, "please be there when I get off, please be there when I get off, please, please, please."

Miriam, who'd been phoned by the worried Mr Grant, was there to meet him as he stepped down from the bus.

"Oscar?" Adam asked weakly.

His mother didn't reply. She simply crouched down and wrapped her arms around him tightly as he started to scream all over again. She looked around her desperately as the bus pulled away. It was looking as though the gradual progress he had made over the previous four years was going to be undone in a single day. It was Miriam's turn to pray.

Please let Oscar be all right, she thought.

"Come on, sonny-Jim," she said as brightly as she could muster. "Let's get some food inside you, some warm clothes on you and we can go and see the fireworks."

"Don't want," murmured Adam. "Don't WANT!" he repeated, screeching the second word. Miriam noticed the net curtain of the house opposite fluttering.

She was tempted to shout something out at the nosy old bag, but there was already enough screaming going on. She heaved the little boy up into her arms and lugged him down the garden path to the house.

They didn't go to the fireworks display that night. Adam was still far too distraught and would only have upset the other children there. Miriam repeated her story that Oscar was just hiding out until the fireworks were all over and then she'd come trotting in, with her tail up in the air, just like always.

"How many fireworks are there then?" Adam asked.

"One million and three," said Miriam, "and when it's

dark we'll go up into the bedroom and watch the rockets, shall we?"

Adam stared sullenly into mid-air.

"Then, we can count them off. And when we've got to a million and three, that's the time Oscar will come back. OK?"

The small boy remained silent. His head was tilted to one side and he slowly twisted his neck round, as if listening out for something. Miriam watched him — all she could hear was the sound of the passing cars and next-door's TV.

"What *are* you listening to, Adam?" she asked.

Unlike all the many times he'd ignored the question, today he turned to look at her.

"The voices," he answered.

"Voices? You mean the television."

"No," he said irritably.

"What voices then?"

"Some like Oscar and some are . . . They're further away. I can't . . ." he frowned in concentration as he twisted his head around again. "I can't hear them properly."

Suddenly a look of complete happiness overwhelmed his worried little face.

"Oscar!" he said quietly and smiled.

Miriam looked at him. If any other child had suddenly claimed to have received confirmation that their pet was alive through some kind of telepathic message, she would have treated it with disbelief. But with her own son she knew better. No one could explain the relationship that had started up the moment Oscar had walked into the house, but the bond between them was indisputable. And while it was impossible to tell *how* the communication between them took place, *that* it took place was never in any doubt. Apart from that, any sort of deception was still difficult for her son. No, if Adam said that Oscar was out there somewhere, she believed him.

"Where is she?"

"Doesn't know," said Adam. "But it's dark — can we go and find her now?"

"It'll be easier in the morning when it's light," said Miriam. She expected him to react to the suggestion, but Adam tilted his head to one side and listened.

"All right," he said finally. "Tomorrow. When all the fireworks have gone."

The first rockets began to whistle and bang at around half past six.

"Hurry," said Miriam, "up to the bedroom."

The two of them raced up the stairs and stood at the window looking out as the explosions of colour splashed across the sky.

"Nineteen, twenty, twenty-one, two, three, twenty-four, five . . . six, seven," Adam called out excitedly as he twisted his head from one side to the other, counting off the red, silver and green rockets as they sparkled, dripped and flashed above the roofs of the houses for a second before disappearing. And Miriam looked down at him, marvelling at the fact that the tiny child who had seemed totally cut off from the outside world had ever learned to count at all.

Adam slept much better that night and the following morning he was up and dressed before it was fully light.

"Come on, Mum," he said, pestering her mercilessly as she cleared away the breakfast bits and pieces. "Come on!"

"All right," she said, abandoning the dishes in the sink and drying her hands. "You win."

Derek had suggested that she should take the car that morning. He would get to Dimwell's by taxi. Even though he found it so difficult to show how he really felt, Miriam had known that he'd been just as worried about the boy as she had.

"Put your jacket on," she said. "It's freezing out."

At that moment the school bus beeped its horn outside. Miriam ran down the path to tell the driver that Adam wouldn't be going to school that day. Then, having scraped the ice off the car windscreen, the pair of them set off.

"Any idea which way to go?" Miriam asked.

Adam shook his head.

"Doesn't work like that," he said.

"Never mind," Miriam said encouragingly. "I'll drive around and you let me know if you hear anything."

She drove slowly to the end of their long road and turned left down towards the centre of town. It began to sleet heavily and Miriam turned the windscreen wipers full on.

"Could be a white Christmas," she said.

But Adam didn't hear. He was twisting his head round from this side to that, listening out for any trace of the missing cat.

"Anything?" she asked.

"Not yet," said Adam.

She turned right at the traffic-lights and circled the pedestrian precinct. The first Santa Claus and Rudolph decorations were already up in the larger department stores.

They get earlier every year, Miriam thought.

Having driven along the delivery road at the back of the main shopping-area, Miriam emerged on to the main by-pass. Passing the industrial estate on her left, she turned right at the roundabout. It occurred to her that they were now on the road leading to Dimwell's, the experimental institute where Derek worked. The awful suspicions she'd had before came back to her.

He couldn't have, she reassured herself. Could he?

It was just before the turn-off to the left that Adam jerked his head around.

"Down there," he yelled excitedly.

Without questioning his instructions, Miriam did as she was told; slammed the brakes on and turned right into the alley-way he was pointing to. A hundred yards further on, it opened up into a concreted area full of garages, some being used as studios, some as repair shops. As they entered the courtyard even Miriam could hear the frantic sound of a cat's plaintive mewing. Adam started running towards a garage in the corner of the yard and as he got there, Miriam saw a dirty, tabby paw reaching out through the gap under the chained door.

"Oscar!" Adam yelled.

"Oscar, you stupid cat, how did you get in there?" Miriam asked, laughing with relief at having found the missing pet. "Adam," she said, "you grab hold of her front legs and I'll pull the door up a fraction. When I say 'now', try to get her through the gap."

She bent down, put her hands under the wooden doors and braced herself.

"Now!"

Miriam heaved, Adam pulled and Oscar appeared. She was looking somewhat scrawny, her fur was matted and totally covered in dirt, but she was alive. And as Adam hugged her tightly she began purring. The loudest she had ever purred. She sounded like a generator.

'Are you all right?' Adam asked.

'I will be,' Oscar said, 'when I've had something to eat and got myself cleaned up a bit.'

'What were you doing there?'

'You know how much I hate the rain. It started pouring down and I thought I'd take shelter. Next thing I knew I'd been locked up.'

'But what were you doing so far from home?' Adam asked. 'Where had you been?'

Oscar shuddered involuntarily.

'I was looking for my . . . for my . . .' she hesitated.

'Yes?' Adam said. Feeling how deeply sad Oscar was, he was beginning to feel uneasy.

'Oh, it's not so important,' said Oscar, 'I'll tell you another time. All that matters now is that you've rescued me. Well done, Adam. Well done!'

—5—

A CHAPTER OF ACCIDENTS

To call Oscar accident-prone would perhaps be an overstatement, but it was certainly the case that she seemed to be getting the maximum amount of mileage out of her nine lives. She had got off to a bad start as a kitten. Born to an old cat in a family where they didn't want any more pets, the owner had roughly bundled the litter of five into a sack and gone off to drown them. It was only because it had started to rain before he'd got to the quarry that he'd dumped the sackful of kittens on the railway embankment, where the two boys on their BMXs had found them the following day. Miriam had chosen Oscar and life number one had been saved.

The greenhouse incident had been altogether more stupid. Oscar had been the equivalent of nine years old at the time and, like any nine-year-old child, was showing off.

'See that bird?' she'd thought, nodding towards a thrush rooting around for worms on the flower-bed. 'I bet I could catch it.'

'Oh don't, Os,' Adam protested. 'I like birds.'

'So do I,' Oscar thought back, licking her lips.

'That's not what I meant,' he retorted. 'Anyway, you get enough food out of tins without having to kill.'

'Cans aren't as much fun,' Oscar replied, beginning to stalk the bird which, oblivious to the attentions of its predator, continued stabbing into the earth.

'Oscar!' Adam warned, but the cat ignored him.

"Shoo! Shoo!" Adam shouted and clapped his hands.

The startled bird flapped its wings and was gone. Oscar looked up at Adam, eyes narrowed.

'Spoil-sport!'

'Well, you shouldn't. You don't need to.'

'It's in my nature,' Oscar thought back sullenly.

'Then chase something unpleasant,' Adam thought. 'Not the birds.'

'Like what? A car? A dog? You?'

Adam didn't answer.

'Didn't mean it,' Oscar thought, regretting her meanness instantly.

'What about that wasp?' Adam suggested, flapping one away from his face.

'Bit small,' the cat sniffed dismissively.

'Bit fast, you mean.'

'You think so, huh? A piece of cake, I can assure you,' and she leapt off after the buzzing insect.

Every time it landed Oscar would pounce. Every time she thought she had caught it, the wasp would spiral up from the cat's paws, hovering for a second around her head before flying off.

From weed to rotten apple, from fence-post to greenhouse,

the wasp flew. As Oscar prepared to launch herself off from a nearby branch, Adam suddenly feared the worst.

"Be c—" he yelled.

But the cat had already flown off into mid-air. Instead of gracefully alighting on the greenhouse roof as she'd intended, she came crashing ingloriously through the glass with a panicked "myaaooow", and landed awkwardly on her two front legs in the middle of the tomatoes. To add insult to injury, while she was lying there mewing, with her useless dislocated legs making it impossible to defend herself, the wasp flew down after her and stung her on the nose.

And though she recovered fully, the vet had insisted she be confined to her basket for three whole weeks.

Then there had been the time when only the quick reactions of old Mr Bailey had prevented her from drowning in the next-door neighbour's pond — the goldfish she had been tormenting for years nearly got their own back! And on another occasion, when a bedraggled and blooded Oscar limped home with lead-shot in her neck and thigh, it had taken the doctor nearly two hours to extract all the tiny pellets from her body. Everyone assumed that the boys from the estate had shot at her with an air-rifle. Oscar explained to Adam that it had been Major Barry, but as there was only the cat's word for it — which only Adam could hear — the unpleasant old man couldn't be taken to court. And then, in addition, there were the innumerable occasions when Oscar had almost lost her life trying to get from one side of the road to the other. However good she might be at mousing, stalking, fishing, climbing or purring, Oscar was a complete dullard at crossing roads.

The next time when her life was seriously in danger, it really hadn't been her fault at all. If anyone was to blame, it was Derek — although perhaps it would be fairer to say that the whole episode merely went to prove that even the simplest of actions is never without its consequences.

It was late spring: Adam had just had his sixth birthday and the slugs were out in force. Although the two events seem totally separate, there was a connection. Adam's grandma had come to wish him happy birthday that afternoon and had brought him an encyclopaedia of animals and a big bag of Dolly Mixtures. In his bedroom that evening, he had lain on the floor comparing the pictures in the book with the wooden animals in his Ark, sharing the sweets with Oscar. The cat particularly liked the hard little white ones and when, a couple of days later, she found similar pellets all round the young lettuce and tomato plants in the garden, it was like having a birthday treat all of her own.

She did notice that they weren't quite as sweet as the Dolly Mixtures, but the taste really wasn't bad at all. And when she started feeling sick soon after, it didn't occur to her that she might have poisoned herself. It was only when she started trembling uncontrollably before collapsing in a heap that Miriam realized something was seriously wrong and the vet was called again.

A foul-tasting antidote, rest in a dark room and lots of sleep gradually led to her recovery.

"Stupid animals," said Derek.

"You're the stupid one," said Miriam. "It says on the packet that Metaldehyde is dangerous for pets."

"Well, what am I supposed to do?" Derek asked angrily. "Let the slugs just eat all the vegetables. Hmm? Maybe I should put a sign up — free lettuce at the Williams' place," he added sarcastically.

"I think a bit of wire netting would have been more effective," she said, equalling her husband's cutting tone. "You might have killed Oscar."

"It's only a cat," Derek shouted. "We could have got a new one."

"Keep your voice down," she said, under her breath. "You know as well as I do that Adam has been a changed character since Oscar arrived."

"Nonsense," said Derek. "Any change would have happened anyway."

"How do you know?"

"We've done endless research into animals and the speech centres in their brains," he said, sounding bored with the whole issue.

Miriam came very close to saying exactly what she thought about the work he did at Dimwell's Institute. The more she thought about it, the more she hated the idea of all the animal experiments that went on there. But she kept her thoughts to herself. Adam seemed so close to animals that the last thing she wanted to do was upset him by letting him know just what his father did.

"There is no evidence at all," Derek continued, "that humans and animals can effectively communicate – whatever a couple of dotty pensioners might claim about the special understanding they've got with Tiddles or Fido. Or even Oscar," he added.

"Oh, I see," she said. "If the great God *Science* has spoken, then it must be true. Not that scientists have ever been wrong about anything before – the world was flat once, the stars revolved around the earth once, thalidomide was safe once . . . Do I have to go on?"

"You're getting hysterical," he said patronizingly.

Miriam resisted the urge to scream at him that it was hardly surprising she lost her temper when he acted and talked so arrogantly, but she bit her tongue and smiled. She would *not* let him upset her.

"It's time for Oscar's medicine," she said, and left.

Adam had been crouched down in the kitchen next to Oscar's sick bed. He had learnt that it was best to keep out of the way when his parents were arguing. But he couldn't help hearing and he wondered what sort of experiments they could possibly do on animals' brains. One thing was certain: whatever they did do at the institute, It was causing yet another argument at home. And for that reason, if for none other, it must be bad!

'Why don't they get on better?' he asked.

'I don't know,' Oscar replied.

'It'd be a lot better if they could think-talk like us,' he thought to Oscar. 'Whenever they use proper words, it all goes wrong somehow.'

'Words are all they've got,' thought Oscar.

"Ah, there you both are," said Miriam, coming into the kitchen carrying the bottle of antidote. "Time for your medicine!"

'Ugh!' Oscar thought, and turned her head away.

'Don't be a baby,' Adam instructed. 'The sooner you take it, the sooner you'll get better.'

And Oscar did get well again. Despite his initial objections, Derek put wire netting over the vegetables to keep Oscar away from the slug pellets. To be honest though, he needn't have bothered. There was no way that the cat would ever go near a slug pellet again – or, for that matter, another Dolly Mixture.

When the most serious threat to her life occurred, however, at the end of a happy summer holiday with Adam, it had nothing to do with poison or bullets or water or traffic. Living in the town, as they did, it was something that none of the Williams' family would have even considered a danger.

Adam's school broke up in July. By this time, Adam was nine and Oscar had reached the equivalent age of forty and a bit. And yet no one would have guessed, seeing the cat tumbling around like a young kitten, that Oscar had officially reached middle age. It was a long, hot summer and to make the days even longer, Adam was getting up at four-thirty or five in the morning, as day broke. Having slipped into jeans and a jumper, he would creep downstairs and out through the back door with Oscar.

They would go through the back gate, across the alley and slide through a gap in the fence to the park. It was a wonderful feeling being the only person there, knowing that the rest of the world was still asleep. The first dog owners only started to appear at around half past six, by which time both Adam and Oscar were feeling hungry and ready to go back home. Miriam was surprised to see her son marching up the garden path at seven o'clock on the first morning of the holiday. She'd assumed he was still in bed. But she didn't mind him playing over in the park in the early morning – the yobs and flashers she worried about preferred the evenings. They were never up that early.

"Well, that was an early start," she said, handing him the box of Sugar Puffs.

"It's the best time," said Adam.

"I'll remind you of that when you're back at school," Miriam said to him. "You never want to get up then."

"'s different," he replied, slurping.

"Evidently," she said, with a grin.

If Miriam had assumed that the dawn starts would be a passing phase that Adam would literally soon tire of, she was wrong. In fact, if anything, he started getting up even earlier. Sometimes, he'd take his Frisbee with him – when the wind was right it worked like a boomerang. On other days, when it was clear and calm, he would go armed with his portable recorder to tape the gradual build up of the birds' dawn chorus. Even on the odd occasions when it rained he wasn't deterred, but went splashing round the stream in his wellies, trying to catch sticklebacks and newts.

It was a Frisbee day when the accident happened. Oscar had wandered off to explore as Adam was throwing it higher and higher, becoming increasingly accurate at judging angle and wind speed so that the disc would come right back to his hands without him having to move at all. If Oscar hadn't been downwind, Adam would have heard her agonized yelps immediately, but as she cried out, the sounds of pain were carried away at once. Higher the Frisbee flew, and still it came spinning back to Adam's outstretched fingers. And then up it soared again, the highest yet as Adam tossed it with all the strength he could muster.

As it began its descent however, the wind suddenly dropped and Adam had to run forwards to try to get underneath it.

"Myyyaaaooowww!" he heard; the sound of the cat screaming echoing all round the park.

"OSCAR!" Adam screamed, abandoning the Frisbee and careering down the hill to the woods where the high-pitched yowling was coming from.

"Where are you? Where are you?" he yelled, rushing frantically through the trees.

"Myyyyaaaiii!" the cat screeched.

"Oscar!" Adam called out again, turning round as he heard a noise behind him.

The cat was now only whimpering quietly, and Adam realized she must be very close. Suddenly he caught sight of Oscar over by the wall at the edge of the park. She was being pinned to the ground by a larger animal.

At first, he thought it must be a dog — but as he looked carefully, he noticed the long, pointed snout and characteristic white front of a fox. It had bitten into Oscar's side and was snarling up at Adam possessively.

"Let her go!" the boy yelled out.

But the bristling fox merely bared its teeth and shook the mewing body.

Adam was so furious that he wanted to jump forward, rip the fox's jaw open. But as he moved, the fox backed away a little and Adam was frightened it would run off with Oscar in its mouth — although it wasn't that much bigger than the cat, it was far more powerfully built.

The boy stood there, totally powerless in the situation.

'Please let my cat go,' he thought desperately. 'Don't hurt her any more.'

The fox cocked its head to one side and as Adam continued to look down, his head was filled with a new voice. It was gruffer than Oscar's silky way of think-speaking, but just as clear and easy to understand.

'Why should I?'

'Because I'm asking you to,' Adam thought back simply. 'She wouldn't do you any harm.'

'She was after my cubs,' the fox retorted.

Adam knew that this was a possibility. Oscar would chase anything that moved — mice, birds, even the occasional rabbit had been cornered and slowly played with to death.

'She won't hurt them,' Adam persisted.

'Not now, she won't,' the fox agreed, letting the limp body drop down to the ground in front of it.

'No,' said Adam quietly.

As he stepped forward and crouched down beside the bleeding body, everything seemed to be moving in slow motion. He lifted the cat's head gently and began tickling her lightly behind the ear.

"Oscar, Oscar," he said in the same low, dazed voice. "Oscar."

'Strange state of affairs it seems to me,' the fox thought to Adam. 'Humans love cats, take them into their homes and feed them — but they hate foxes. Gas us, poison us, shoot us, they do.'

'You're wrong,' thought Adam. 'Oscar's been shot too. There are some people who like cats *and* foxes. And some who just don't seem to like animals at all.'

'Perhaps you're right,' the fox conceded.

'Anyway,' Adam continued indignantly, 'if you're so sure that humans do hate foxes, what are you doing living in the middle of a town.'

'It wasn't by choice,' the fox thought back. 'This whole area used to be farmland — it's only recently that all your houses were built. Where were we meant to move to?'

'Well, out into the country.'

'Impossible,' the fox claimed. 'It all happened so fast, we were surrounded. And, anyway, living on the land isn't all it's cracked up to be these days. Gamekeepers put down poisoned eggs to trick us so that we can't kill their pheasants — so that they can shoot them instead,' it added, snorting bitterly.

Adam listened miserably, continuing to stroke away at Oscar's lifeless body.

'Farmers shoot us although we do more good than harm, keeping down rodents, slugs and beetles. Shepherds say we kill lambs, but all we do is carry off the bodies of those that were born dead. And as for the hunting men and women with their red coats and shiny horns, they come galloping across the fields on their horses with packs of hounds, claiming they need to keep our numbers down. It's a nightmare. We're really not *that* bad at all — just mis-understood.'

Adam had switched off from the fox's diatribe.

'You've killed Oscar,' he thought miserably. 'She's dead.'

'She's not dead,' the fox thought back. 'I can see her breathing. No, on balance,' it added, returning to its theme, 'life is considerably easier in the towns. Infinitely safer on the whole and there's such an easy food supply – humans throw away an awful lot of food, you know.'

But Adam wasn't listening any longer. At first, lost in his numbing misery, the fox's throwaway remark hadn't registered. But then, as he looked more carefully at Oscar's pathetic little body, he realized that her chest was indeed moving.

'You're alive,' Adam whispered into her ear.

The cat whimpered pitifully.

'Oh, Oscar,' Adam thought. 'I was so sure that . . .'

He picked her up carefully and cradled her over one crooked arm, continuing to stroke her with the other hand. And as he walked back across the park, the fox trotted along beside him, telling him story after foxy story as it did so. Arriving at the hole in the fence behind his house, Adam pushed the movable slat to one side. The fox declined to come through with him.

'I think I'll just bid you farewell here and now, if you don't mind.'

'OK,' Adam thought back. The fox had been painting such a horrific picture of what humans could and would do to foxes if they saw them during the day that he could well understand the animal's reluctance to go any further.

'I'd just like to say that it's been a pleasure talking to you like this,' the fox thought to Adam. 'I'd heard stories, you know, about there being some humans who could communicate with us animals, but I'd put them all down to rumours and legends, much like the ones I've been telling you, but now I know I was wrong. The gift evidently hasn't been entirely lost. And I'm glad.'

'So am I,' Adam thought back, and meant it. Meeting the fox had answered so many questions that he couldn't wait for Oscar to get better again so that he could talk about everything with her.

'And I'm very sorry about your cat,' the fox added.

'I know you are,' thought Adam. 'She'll be all right.'

And with that, the fox trotted back to the hollow where it had left its sleeping cubs, while Adam slipped through the gap in the fence. He walked down the garden path as fast as he possibly could without hurting Oscar. His mum was there in the kitchen, reading the paper.

"Mummy," he said, holding up the injured animal.

"Oh, good lord," said Miriam, "that cat!" And she rushed off to telephone the vet once again.

"Hold on, Os," Adam whispered.

The cat whimpered weakly.

"For me. Please, hold on."

—6—
MAMMALOGUE

It was touch and go for a long while. The vet did all he could, stitching up the worst wounds and prescribing an ointment to keep out infection. But during Oscar's recovery, there were several occasions when no one expected her to pull through. For no apparent reason she would suddenly start shivering convulsively. There was nothing they could do then except make sure the kitchen where she was sleeping was nice and warm, and keep their fingers crossed.

During the weeks of waiting for Oscar to recover, Adam gradually got used to the fact that at some stage his feline companion was no longer going to be around. The incident with the fox had made that fact slightly easier to bear. Not only had he discovered that it wasn't only Oscar that he could think-speak to, but he had found out that at one time there were lots of other humans who had been able to do the same. Man had all but lost the ability so that Adam, far from being seen as a major talent in the art of animal communication, had been diagnosed mentally ill and treated as a freak.

"But how is it different?" his mother had asked him.

"It's difficult to explain," said Adam. "That's the problem. If an animal asked me that, I could just think back the answer perfectly and it would understand — feelings, meaning, definition. But when I speak to you and other people I have to think first, then find the nearest words to those thoughts, then say them."

"But thoughts are in words, aren't they?" Miriam said.

"Well, sort of," said Adam and laughed. "You see, when I've said the words, then I need to explain what I *really* mean. And sometimes I just can't. It's all very slow and haphazard."

"And you don't know how you learned to talk to animals like that?" Miriam said.

"I didn't have to learn — it was something I could always do," he said. "Like breathing. It was learning to listen to people that was so difficult. Tuning in to the clumsy, ugly mess of sounds — and then even harder to try and copy them."

"You've managed it though, haven't you?" said Miriam warmly, giving her son a big hug. She didn't care whether it *was* all in his mind. The undeniable fact was that, every day, Adam was improving.

"You've managed it just fine."

With Oscar laid up for so long, Adam was to discover that although the cat had offered him the key to communication, she had also locked the door on his discovering too much. On that very first meeting with the boy when she'd rubbed her paws down him, she had claimed Adam for herself. And since then, true to her word, she had guarded him jealously, keeping all potential intruders away. Often, while Adam was asleep in bed, he would be woken by the sound of cats fighting, and the cuts and scratches that Oscar would be sporting the following day confirmed what she had been up to. And as for the other animals that lived near by, the only ones to actually get inside the garden were dead ones, carried in triumphantly between Oscar's jaws.

In the six months or so that Oscar was confined to the kitchen, the neighbouring animals — both wild and tame — came to forget the infamous defender, and ventured inside the forbidden garden. To his astonishment, Adam found that he was able to think-speak with all the mammals he met.

The first in were other cats. As the territorial scent that Oscar would leave on the fence-posts and corners of the garage gradually faded, the neighbourhood cats came to investigate.

'She's ill,' Adam would explain. 'A fox got her.'

And the other cats would tut and miaow sympathetically.

'Of course,' a tortoise shell from a few doors down told him, 'we'd all heard that there was a boy living here who could talk to us, but Mingwaal was so possessive that she'd never let us near you.'

'Mingwaal,' Adam repeated. 'I'd forgotten that was her real name. I think she said it meant Protector.'

'That's right. And she certainly lived up to her name as far as you were concerned.'

'She was just jealous,' a Siamese-tom retorted as it slunk round Adam's legs. 'If you'd met me, you'd have been sure to have got rid of the old scruff-bucket. I've always thought tabby was so *common*,' it added, pompously.

'I wouldn't have,' Adam thought back indignantly.

'Ah, loyalty, a splendid trait,' the tortoise shell noted. 'Uh-oh,' she thought, looking up at a sleek black cat which had just leapt on to the garage roof at the end of the garden. 'Here comes trouble!'

'How do you mean?' Adam asked.

'Bit of a bully,' the tortoiseshell whispered back.

It occurred to Adam that just as the people he met were all so different, the characters of the cats he met were equally diverse. He'd heard his father say that people's pets came to be like their owners – from his own experience he thought that the opposite was more likely true. Owners of bulldogs would gradually become stubborn and dogmatic, owners of snowy-white Persians would inevitably get vainer by the day, while the boy down the road with the tortoise was without doubt the slowest individual he'd ever met. He realized that he'd have to analyse Oscar's character very carefully if he wanted to understand himself better.

'I hope you're defending our territory while I'm ill,' Oscar thought to Adam one evening.

'Of course I am,' Adam replied, not quite truthfully.

'It's a pity you haven't got scent glands,' she added ruefully.

Apart from the cats, the occasional wild animal would come to visit. A shrew, a bat, a couple of squirrels and a family of hedgehogs all made themselves known to the small boy who could communicate with the animals.

As they weren't exactly *talking*, Adam couldn't tell what their voices were like, but in the same way that when the fox had been think-speaking it had been gruff, so he would describe the shrew's thoughts as shrill, the bat's as vibrato and the squirrels' as chattery.

Of all the wild animals he met, the most likeable were the visitors he spotted one evening. At first, hearing the sound of her saucer being knocked about, Adam had assumed Oscar was getting better. But when he looked down he saw that a small, prickly animal was snouting about in the cat food. Miriam had put the saucer outside the door while she was cleaning, forgotten all about it and now a hedgehog was helping itself to the tinned meat.

'There's something eating my dinner now,' Oscar protested feebly as Adam passed through the kitchen.

'I'm just going to investigate.'

'I don't know. Give them an inch . . .' he heard Oscar muttering to herself.

"Hey!" Adam called out as the little animal scurried away, startled by the sound of the back door. 'Don't run,' he thought. 'I won't hurt you.'

The hedgehog re-emerged from its concealed corner under the privet bush. It looked around and sniffed at the air suspiciously, threatening to roll up into a tight ball at the first hint of danger.

'Was that you?'

Adam nodded.

'Well I never, how wonderful!' the hedgehog thought excitedly. 'Incredible!'

'What is?' he asked, crouching down beside the little animal.

It wasn't that Adam was becoming blasé about being able to talk to animals, but rather that as the animals themselves seemed so unimpressed by the phenomenon, he too had stopped thinking about how wonderful it was. The hedgehog, unlike the cats and the squirrels and the foxes, was clearly beside itself with surprise and delight.

'But do you realize how we're communicating?' it quizzed Adam.

'Well, think-speaking,' he answered, using the word that Oscar had given him.

'But the fact that we can actually understand each other,' the hedgehog persisted.

Adam shrugged.

'This is Mammalogue,' it said.

'Mammalogue?' Adam repeated. 'What's that?'

'He doesn't even know,' the hedgehog thought to no one in particular. 'Amazing!'

And it proceeded to tell the boy all about the language which had come into existence millions and millions of years earlier. Blinding, or rather deafening Adam with science, it rattled off the names of the different geological eras and periods, listing the development of life on earth from the early, pre-Cambrian worms and sponges, through the Silurian fish, Carboniferous reptiles and on to the Triassic period of the Mesozoic era, when the dinosaurs were in their heyday.

Then, as the massive, stupid beasts were lumbering about eating everything they could, small, furry, warm-blooded creatures came into existence. Dodging out of the way of the huge, dangerous dinosaurs was no easy matter and the tiny creatures needed all the help they could give one another. A way of transferring messages instantly from one to the other became essential and it was for this purpose that a brand-new form of communication came into existence. And that communication was Mammalogue.

'But what . . .?'

'Don't interrupt,' the hedgehog thought back, 'I haven't finished yet. Of course,' it continued, 'the periods progressed, and the Cretaceous moved into the Palaeocene, which switched to the Eocene and on to the Oligocene and so forth, and the mammals divided and sub-divided into Chiroptera, Edentata, Carnivora, Cetacea, Insectivora – like me, and primates, like you, and gradually Mammalogue fell into disuse. The dinosaurs died out and new, specialized languages developed – horses learnt *horse*, and whales learnt *whale*. After all, it would have been off-putting if, just as a lion was about to kill an antelope, its dinner turned round and said: "Please don't eat me."'

'But you said . . .' Adam tried again.

'I'm still not ready yet,' the hedgehog snapped back. 'Anyway, *even though* mammals lost the need to use

Mammalogue, and *even though* most of them forgot that once upon a time they had all been able to communicate with each other, the ability remains. And, for some reason, you've been born with that same ability.'

The hedgehog took a deep breath.

'Now what were you going to ask me?'

Adam couldn't remember. The thoughts – the *Mammalogue* thoughts – that the hedgehog had filled his head with were all spinning round chaotically. An ancient language. Over a hundred million years old! It was all too much to take in.

'Oh dear,' thought the hedgehog. 'I didn't mean to alarm you, I was just . . .'

'No, it's all right,' Adam thought back reassuringly. He looked around and noticed the saucer lying upside down. 'Would you, er . . . like a bit more to eat?'

'Wouldn't say no.'

'You like milk, don't you?'

'Bit of a myth, that one,' the hedgehog replied. 'We're actually much more partial to pet food.'

'As you like,' Adam thought back, and took the saucer in for a refill.

'Where are you going with that?' Oscar asked, weakly trying to raise her head.

'Nowhere.'

'Must be going somewhere,' Oscar grumbled. 'And now you're taking it outside for nothing to eat it, I suppose,' she thought miserably as Adam walked back past her.

"I'll be back in a minute," he said.

'Hmmph,' the cat thought and lowered her head back on to the cushion – the least exercise tired her out.

'There you go,' said Adam as he put the saucer down and watched, fascinated, as the hedgehog rapidly polished off the heap of meaty chunks.

'Very nice,' thought the hedgehog, having flipped the saucer over in search of a juicy worm it might have for dessert.

'So you really don't like milk then?' Adam asked. 'At school we were told to put down a saucerful if we wanted to attract hedgehogs into the garden.'

'I know,' it said. 'The number of times I've found a little dish that someone's left out and all it's got in it is bread and milk. It's so disappointing. I can't digest the stuff at all,' it explained, 'it gives me the runs. There have been so many misconceptions about hedgehogs over the centuries,' it continued.

Adam sat down next to the animal. 'Like what?'

'Oh, stupid things,' it thought. 'Humans used to believe that at harvest-time we'd climb up a vine or a tomato plant, knock down some fruit and then roll over it so it would stick to the prickles. Sort of spearing it, like on the end of a fork. Then we were meant to trot home to our young ones, all done up like a fruit salad, for a nice little snack.'

Adam laughed at the thought of a bunch of grapes on legs rushing through the undergrowth.

'Ridiculous,' the hedgehog continued, 'what would happen if *you* rolled over a tomato?'

'I'd squash it.'

'Precisely. And we're meant to kill snakes like that as well – rolling over them, piercing their skin and ripping the flesh from the bones. Total nonsense. If *I* see a snake, I get out of the way pretty sharpish.

'Oh, and there was another ridiculous story going round. We always used to get on well with farmers – we ate the slugs, caterpillars, beetles which damaged their crops, and they left us alone. Then someone started circulating this ridiculous rumour that we drank the cows' milk – straight from the udder. As I said, I don't even *like* milk. I stopped drinking it when I was six weeks old. No, I don't know what it is about humans, but they really do like telling the tallest stories. And the crazy thing is that however far-fetched, however implausible, there is *always* someone fool enough to believe them.'

'I'll tell you what,' Adam thought to the hedgehog, 'one thing that they wouldn't believe is that you and I can communicate.'

'No,' the hedgehog sighed, 'that's because humans have moved so far away from the animals. And it's sad, because the further they remove themselves the less they understand, and the less they understand the more havoc they wreak.'

'How do you mean?'

'Everything in nature is interdependent,' the hedgehog explained. 'There is a delicate balance on earth between predators and prey, but humans don't seem able to grasp how it works and they keep ruining the food-chain. And as sure as eggs is eggs, it'll end in disaster.'

'But everything *seems* OK,' Adam countered, looking round the garden and over at the back where the tall trees were swaying in the twilight breeze.

'Granted. But just below the surface . . . Let me try to make it simple. Look, your father grows roses, but he doesn't like it when there are greenfly on them, does he? So what does he do?'

'Sprays them.'

'He sprays them,' the hedgehog repeated. 'So he's managed to get rid of the greenfly, but he's also killed the ladybirds and hoverflies which prey off them. When the greenfly return, and they always do, there are no predators to limit their numbers. What happens then? They multiply more than ever. So he sprays them again, and when it rains the poison gets into the soil and into the earthworms and the weevils. And what eats them? The robins and blackbirds, weasels and stoats, foxes and – hedgehogs, of course. The chemicals gradually filter through the whole food-chain, poisoning all of it. That pet food you just gave me was probably the healthiest meal I've had in months. And all because humans like roses without greenfly on them.'

Adam was beginning to feel unpleasantly guilty and vowed that when *he* grew up, he would never use any pesticides, insecticides, herbicides or any other 'nasticide' in the garden.

'The irony of it is,' the hedgehog continued relentlessly, 'that the greenfly themselves are all becoming immune to the sprays. They're not like mammals. In the end, the insects will probably be the only living creatures left on earth.'

"Adam," Miriam called out. "What are you doing?"

"Coming," he shouted back.

'I've got to go,' he thought to the hedgehog. 'I'll put some more food down for you.'

'Well, I'll be hibernating soon, but that would be very nice for the next couple of nights.'

'I'll try and get out to see you.'

'Well, if you can't,' the hedgehog thought, 'don't forget how important your ability to use Mammalogue is. Even though it's not clear why you can as yet, I'm certain that everything will be revealed as you grow older. Make sure you don't squander your gift.'

'I won't,' Adam promised.

'Oh, and by the way,' the hedgehog added, 'I'm rather partial to the occasional pilchard!'

—7—
LITTERS OF KITTENS

Oscar's complete recovery took considerably longer than anyone had expected. And while she was slowly but surely gaining strength, life was going on as usual outside. The hedgehog went into hibernation for three months and re-emerged the following spring to mate, the squirrels raised two separate litters of young, while the neighbourhood cats, who had all but forgotten that the Williams' garden was Oscar's territory, would come in heavy with kittens one month, unladen the next. It wasn't until the middle of June that the vet pronounced Oscar herself healthy enough to venture outside.

'I thought I'd never be well again,' she sighed, as she trotted through the back door.

That first night when Oscar was allowed to stay out, Adam lay in bed awake, listening to the sound of protracted caterwauling followed by furious bursts of frenzied attack.

He knew then that it'd been absolutely right to limit the cat's freedom until she was fully recovered.

It took Oscar three nights to reclaim the garden for herself and luckily she didn't have anything worse than a cut ear to show for her troubles.

'You're nothing but a bully,' Adam said, sitting on the floor and letting the cat rub her head possessively over his knees and arms. 'You realize that all the visitors I've been having will stop coming now. They're all afraid of you.'

Oscar merely purred all the louder.

Everything was finally back to normal. Or at least, on the surface it was. As another summer drifted into another autumn, however, they both realized that something had indeed changed. Something which neither of them wanted to mention, but which, as the weeks passed, occupied their thoughts increasingly often. In the end it was a regular check-up at the vet's that confirmed what they had both suspected all along. The bite inflicted by the fox had damaged Oscar internally and she would never have any more young.

Not that she had done badly. Over the years, she had given birth to a grand total of forty-three kittens. But nevertheless, both Oscar and Adam were saddened by the news that there would be no more excited waiting as Oscar's nine-week pregnancies gradually approached the day when she would produce her litter of tiny, mouse-like babies.

'Do you remember what we called them all?' Adam asked her, as they were both sitting up on his bed.

'I remember *my* names for them,' she said, reminding Adam that pets have both a human and a species name. 'I'm not sure I can remember all the things you called them. There was Eeny, Meeny, Miney and Mo, wasn't there?'

'Yes, and Snowy, Blackie, Patch, Smudge and Whiskers.'

'Nik, Nak, Paddy and Wak.'

'Parsley, Sage, Rosemary and Thyme.'

They both sat there thinking – surely they couldn't have forgotten the other names.

'Oh yes,' Adam remembered, 'Tom, Dick and Harry.'

Silence again.

'And . . . and . . .'

'Yes?'

'No, it's gone. Parsley, Sage – no, I said them.'

Try as hard as they could, none of the other names would come back. And yet when they had been born, the kittens had all been so individually important that Adam had never imagined he could ever forget them.

'Come on then,' he said finally. 'What did *you* call them?'

And as he listened Oscar, or Mingwaal as she was really called, reeled off the names. Adam closed his eyes and listened to the strangely feline sounds that filled his head. He couldn't prove it, of course, but he knew that Oscar wouldn't lie about anything so close to her – she remembered every single one of the kittens.

'Lovely names,' Adam thought to Oscar.

'Much nicer than Tom, Dick and Harry anyway,' Oscar thought back.

'I wonder where they all are now,' he thought.

'I wonder.'

Something about the way she had repeated the words made Adam look up. Oscar was gazing out through the window at the leaves falling thickly from the trees like a red and yellow blizzard. Her silence made Adam feel uneasy.

'What is it?' he asked.

'Nothing. I was just wondering where they all are now as well.'

'I'm sure they're all in really nice homes,' Adam thought back encouragingly. 'Dad always promised that they'd be well looked after, didn't he?'

'He did,' Oscar conceded. 'He did.'

Her bitter sadness was unmistakable.

'Oscar,' Adam thought, 'what is it?'

'Oh, I don't know,' she thought. 'I don't want to accuse anyone unfairly, but . . . well, you know where your father works, don't you? Dimwell's Research Institute. And, you know what they do there . . Well, maybe it's better all round that I don't have any more kittens, that's all.'

Adam knew that feelings of family loyalty ought to make him object to the implications Oscar was making. How dare a mere cat suggest that his father might have in any way harmed the kittens? He should feel righteous indignation. He should feel affronted, insulted and vigorously defend his father's good name whatever the cost to his friendship. And yet he remained silent. Oscar's insinuations had come far too close for comfort to his own fears for the kittens.

It had all started with the conversation with the hedgehog. Learning that the delicate balance of nature could be destroyed by human's stupid use of pesticides and herbicides had frightened him. For weeks afterwards, he'd had a recurring nightmare.

It would always begin in the same way. Adam would be out in the garden on a bright, sunny afternoon. The dazzling display of flowers – delphiniums, carnations, peonies, alyssum and goldenrod – were all vying for the attention of the bees, who would pollenate them while taking their sweet nectar. But there was one flower which smelled sweeter than the rest. A tall, pure white rose, completely surrounded by bees and butterflies which, intoxicated by the perfume, ignored all the other flowers in the garden. As Adam approached the rose, however, he noticed that other insects had been drawn close too. Green aphids completely covered the stems and leaves, while at the centre of the flower a black worm was slowly eating away at the heart of the petals.

"Kill it, Daddy, kill it!" he would shout, and immediately the whole garden was filled with a choking fog of foul-tasting smoke. It stung his eyes and made him retch emptily.

Gradually, the smoke would disperse, and as Adam opened his eyes the garden had all but disappeared. Stretching away from him in both directions as far as the eye could see was a column of trapped insects, birds and animals. A tight metal ring encircled the neck of every single being, from the tiniest mite at one end, to the colossal blue whale, floundering desperately at the other. And linking each of the animals in between was a second ring, so that the whole wide range of life was joined together in a single chain that shuffled across the earth like a column of prisoners manacled to one another. And as Adam watched, the column got slower and slower as individuals died, fell and were dragged along by those still surviving. Finally, the point was reached when the dead outnumbered the living, who were, in any case, too weak to pull any further. The chain collapsed.

For a while there was silence, apart from the sound of a desolate wind whistling through the motionless chain. Then all at once Adam would notice a scratching, a squeaking, a scurry of movement. At first a feeling of relief would overwhelm him, but an instant later, as he became aware of the cause of this new activity, he would scream in utter terror. Creeping, crawling all over the dead, animating them in a parody of life, were cockroaches. Millions of them. Brown-black and stinking of sewers, they jostled and jockeyed for position as they devoured everything: the animals, the birds, the insects, even the chain itself. A thick, rustling, heaving carpet of ravenous scavengers — and then, when there was nothing else left to eat, their antennae would pick up the presence of Adam.

And he would wake up dripping with sweat and screaming out against the horror.

"It's only a nasty dream," Miriam would say, wiping his brow and stroking his back. "A nasty dream that can't hurt you."

But Adam wasn't convinced. It was so explicit, and the fact that the dream was repeated night after night meant that it began to haunt him during the day too. The words the hedgehog had used about humans kept coming back to him: '. . . the further they remove themselves the less they understand, and the less they understand the more havoc they wreak.'

What if the nightmare wasn't merely his imagination running wild?

What if it was a warning?

He knew that his father would react badly if he asked him anything about the research institute. Miriam even advised him not to. But the more the dream recurred, the more he couldn't *not* ask him. Over the years, as Adam had gradually learnt to communicate better with people, the relationship with his father had settled down to a form of mutual toleration. For Derek's part, he couldn't help remaining disappointed in the son he had ended up with. Although Adam was perhaps less of an idiot, something more than a half-wit these days, every time the boy opened his mouth, his mangling of the spoken word would make Derek wince. From Adam's point of view, things were different. He had no experience of other fathers to compare his own with. Of course, he knew that he embarrassed, frustrated and angered the man, but then perhaps all sons did that. What he did find disturbing about his father was his coldness. There was something so clinical and unfeeling about him. Even his laughter rang hollow.

"Dad?" he said.

"Yes?"

"You know insecticides and weed-killers and things?"

"Not personally."

"Well, do they do any harm?"

"If you're an insect or a weed, yes."

"No, but on other things."

"Like what?"

"Well, animals and birds that eat the insects — hedgehogs, robins . . ."

His father looked at him suspiciously. "Why?"

"It's just that . . . We were doing this project at school," he said, deciding to keep quiet about the hedgehog, "and they said that if you poison all the insects, then the birds that eat them die as well, and then owls and hawks that eat them die, and so do the foxes and badgers, because they're all being poisoned, and in the end they'll all end up dead," he blurted out, suddenly getting all mixed up in his own mind. "And it's not that bad having a few greenfly on your roses, is it?" he added.

Derek put his knife and fork down, and looked first at Miriam and then at Adam.

"I don't know who's been filling your head with this sort of drivel," he suddenly exploded. "A whole load of so-called 'greens', I suppose. Weirdos and loonies, the lot of them. Have you any idea what would happen if we didn't use these pesticides. Have you? Well, have you?"

Adam shook his head meekly.

"You'd have slugs eating the green crops, maggots eating the fruit, wire-worms eating the potatoes, mice eating the wheat and barley. And then what would we have to eat? Huh? I'll tell you what we'd have. Nothing. This wouldn't be here for a start," he shouted, stabbing at a roast potato, "and neither would these, or these," he continued, prodding the peas and broccoli. "This plate would be empty. And you know what would happen then? We'd starve. Curtains. Finish!" — his hand miming a knife slashing through his throat.

"I'm sick to death of namby-pamby, wishy-washy do-gooders who haven't the first idea about science, going on about things they're too stupid to understand."

Adam was shaking. He wanted to scream or run away and hide, or something – anything to stop his father shouting.

'You're doing fine,' came Oscar's voice. 'Ask him how he knows.' She was sitting over on the chair, licking herself clean. But though apparently oblivious to the entire scene, her encouragement and advice proved that she was all ears.

"How do you know?" Adam asked simply.

"How do I know what?" he snapped back.

Adam fell silent. He was feeling increasingly confused.

'How do you know that in the long term, the whole food-chain isn't going to fall apart?' Oscar thought to Adam.

Adam repeated the sentence. Scarcely noticing the sudden improvement in his son's vocabulary and delivery, Derek stood up and shouted his reply.

"Because I'm a scientist. Because it's my business to know."

"But how?"

"We do tests. Experiments," he said, calming down a little. "And the amounts of poisons used are *far* too small to harm anything other than the insects they're designed to eradicate."

"Oh," said Adam, who was prepared to believe that his father knew what he was talking about and that the hedgehog had been mistaken.

Oscar was evidently not convinced however.

'Ask him *how* they know what's dangerous and what's not dangerous to other animals.'

'Oh, Oscar,' Adam protested.

'Ask him!' Oscar insisted.

"And *how* do you know what's dangerous and what's not dangerous to other animals?" he repeated quietly.

"I told you," his father snapped. "We do tests. We know *exactly* how much of every single pesticide, herbicide, insecticide it takes to kill each species and . . ."

As his father spoke, Adam realized with a sudden shock why Oscar had insisted he persist with the questions.

". . . based on that, we *know* that the amounts we use outside are harmless."

"To animals."

"To animals."

"And pets."

"And pets."

"Because you've done tests on them."

"Yes, we've . . ."

Suddenly realizing the trap he'd walked into, Derek's face turned white with fury. Then it reddened, blotchily. He looked around the room at the accusing eyes of his son and wife. Even the cat seemed to be staring at him with a mixture of contempt and loathing.

"I do not have to put up with this," he said calmly, laid his napkin down beside the plate of half-eaten food and left the table.

A moment later, they heard the front door shutting with a click and the car being started.

"Not your kittens," said Miriam, holding the boy who, now the tension was going, had dissolved into tears. "I promise you, angel," she said. "I know he seems a bit cold sometimes, but if he said they were going to good homes, he meant it."

Adam continued to sob uncontrollably, only stopping when he could physically cry no longer. With his wet shirt and dry mouth, it seemed as though he'd completely run out of tears.

Both Adam and Oscar realized that Miriam meant well by reassuring them about the kittens, but neither was really convinced that even she believed what she was saying. They had to see for themselves that none of Oscar's offspring had ended up at the institute.

The following day Adam rushed home after school and, with Oscar in his travel-basket to make the journey quicker, he sneaked out of the house and headed towards the outskirts of town.

Even with the bus, which dropped them off within half a mile of the research institute, the journey had taken the best part of an hour. And as Adam and Oscar stood with their noses pressed against the perimeter fence, they both felt cold and miserable.

'It looks harmless enough, doesn't it?'

'If only we could get a closer look.'

'I don't think that's going to be possible,' said Adam. 'They've got guards, look. With German shepherds.'

'I'd already noticed,' Oscar replied, with a shudder.

Apart from the metal notice on the entrance-gate informing them otherwise, the buildings inside the fenced-in site could have been a school. In the centre was an imposing Victorian mansion with steep slate roofs and tall chimneys – a modern extension had been built on to the east wing. Surrounding the main building was a hotchpotch of prefab buildings, each one made sinister with the thick wire netting covering the windows.

"Dimwell Government Research Institute," Adam read out loud. "Danger. Access to unauthorized personnel strictly prohibited."

Most of the employees had already left for the day and there were only a couple of lights still on in the complex. Adam wondered whether his father was there; wondered what he was doing?

Neither Adam nor Oscar had come armed with any plan of action. They simply wanted to see the place. Even if they had intended to break in, the coiled reels of barbed wire at the top of the fence, the spotlights illuminating the no man's land between the buildings and perimeter wire, the prominent alarm system and the huge uniformed guards patrolling the grounds with their straining dogs were more than enough to convince the boy and his cat that they wouldn't have stood a chance.

Silently looking in through the fence, it was impossible to tell whether this was where the kittens had been brought. All they could do was hope that it hadn't been, for although they were unable to communicate with the animals locked up there, both of them could feel the deathly atmosphere emanating from inside. Adam's head was full of the chaos of lost, lonely and despairing cries and whispers. Oscar turned away; she had called out each of her kittens' names in turn, but apart from the echoing sound of misery she had received back, there had been no sign that they might be there.

'We may as well go,' she thought to Adam.

He nodded. The longer they remained there, the more the hideous atmosphere began to get to them. And though neither of them would acknowledge what was making them shiver and shake, they both knew that it was the unbearable closeness of so much suffering.

It smelled of pain.

It smelled of death.

—8—
NEW STORIES FOR OLD

The cold that Adam caught that evening, standing outside Dimwell's and walking back with the icy wind against him, lasted for over a fortnight. After the initial blocked nose and sneezing stage, it had gone down on to his chest, where it threatened to turn to pneumonia. He was not allowed to go to school and, at home in bed, Oscar was banned from his room as the doctor thought that her fur could aggravate the boy's severe cough.

For the first few days, he didn't want to do anything but sleep. He was cold and shivery, as if the atmosphere of the research institute had infected his whole body, although in his feverish state, he couldn't actually remember anything about his visit to Dimwell's. It was only when his temperature dropped back to normal that the incident which had preceded his illness came back to him.

That awful place, he thought and shuddered, not now with cold, but rather with horror.

His mum seemed determined to let the whole matter drop and whenever she popped up to see how he was, she steadfastly refused to ask anything about his and Oscar's trip.

"Are you feeling better now?" she asked him as she brought him soup and a poached egg on toast.

"Much," he said, sitting up. "I think I could get up."

"The doctor said, not till Sunday," she said, "and he knows best."

Adam just shrugged. If he had to be perfectly honest, he really wasn't minding the stay in bed at all.

"I'll tell you what though," she added. "As you're obviously over the worst now, I think it'll be OK for Oscar to come in tomorrow."

"Not now?"

"No, we'll leave it till tomorrow. Now is there anything you want before I go?"

"My book, please," he said.

Miriam didn't have to ask which book in particular he meant. Although he could read novels, he seldom did. Instead, he had one particular favourite. It was over seven hundred pages long, but Adam knew it inside out. It was the huge encyclopaedia of animal life that his grandmother had bought him for his sixth birthday. At the time, Miriam was sure that it was too adult for him, and she worried that he would scribble all over the pages. But her fears proved totally unfounded. Even though the book had been almost too big and heavy for the boy to open, he'd treated it with the reverence of a scholar with a hand-illustrated medieval volume. And now, some four and a half years on, it still held the same fascination for Adam: a fascination that no other book could equal.

At first, it had been the thousands of photographs that had kept him spellbound as he'd flicked through the pages. Later, as his reading had improved, he'd started to take in some of the captions and annotations. It was only after meeting the hedgehog, however, that he finally sat down to the task of reading the text in its entirety. Totally baffled by the string of words the prickly little animal had used in his explanation of how and why Mammalogue had come into existence, Adam had gone back to the book to check whether he had been using scientific terms, or gibberish. He soon discovered it to be the former. Silurian, Mesozoic, Cretaceous, Chiroptera, Edentata, Cetacea – all the strange words he'd never heard of before were there in black and white. Adam was fascinated. Perhaps there would be some mention of Mammalogue too, he thought, and scoured the entire book for any reference. There was none, but even so, he wasn't disappointed.

He learnt about birds which could weave nests, ants which built homes for themselves out of slices of leaves, eels which could stun their prey with bolts of electricity, molluscs which could see both ultra-violet and infra-red, crickets with ears on their elbows, bats with radar, fish with wings. The encyclopaedia was more wonderful than anything he could ever have imagined.

And as he read on, he discovered the existence of countless peculiar animal pairs. Ants would milk aphids; tiny plovers would hop in and out of crocodiles' mouths, picking their teeth; tick-birds would peck the irritating insects out from the folds of rhinoceroses' skin; while parrot-fish could somehow swim in and out of anemones' deadly tentacles without being harmed. There was a purpose to all these relationships. And they made Adam think.

Why can I speak to the animals? he wondered for the umpteenth time as he laid the book down.

He knew that it *was* just restricted to mammals. Experiments at talking with the birds in the trees, the frogs and fish in the neighbour's pond and a stray tortoise that had wandered through the Williams' garden one afternoon had all proved as fruitless as if he'd been trying to communicate with a plank of wood.

His gift was limited to communicating with those warm-blooded creatures which produce milk for their young.

But why?

Having slept so much over the past few days, he lay in bed that night, wide awake and listening to the distant murmuring chatter he'd been hearing since his birth – the sound of countless million mammals, near and far, all simply *being*.

'What do you want me to do?' he called out into the night. 'Just tell me.'

But once again, he was to drift off to sleep without receiving an answer.

Adam had to admit that, although he moaned about it when he was there, he was missing school now that he was feeling better. Realizing that the boy was, if not obsessed, then certainly preoccupied with animals, the teachers allowed him to pursue his interest as much as he wanted. In this respect, he was lucky to be at a special school, where motivation was more important than guiding the child towards specific examinations. And, in the end, Adam did cover all the ground he would have covered at an ordinary school, but with his own special angle on everything.

In art, his subject matter was animals; in maths, it would be figures to do with gestation periods, life expectancy and size of litters that he would multiply, subtract and divide; and though his history was shaky, his biology was far in advance of his years.

"Adam has an encyclopaedic knowledge of the subject,"

the teachers would tell his mother at parents' evenings — a fact that was hardly surprising.

Where he really excelled was in writing. It was in the autumn following Oscar's fight with the fox that Adam had attempted his first story, and his form-teacher, Mr Thomas, was so impressed with the result that he had entered it for a competition in a local newspaper.

It was called 'The Fox and the Fleas Who Outstayed Their Welcome' and was, not surprisingly, about a somewhat flea-bitten old fox who used all his cunning and slyness to rid himself of the infestation of parasites. Having been unable to reason with the fleas, the fox had held a twist of wool in his teeth and backed slowly into a pond. Fearing that they would drown, the fleas had run up the fox's body and along his snout, until all of them were crowded together on the wool. At the moment when the last of them hopped across from his nose on to the wool, the fox released them all.

And good riddance! he'd thought, as the fleas sailed away on their makeshift raft.

The story was clearly well written and imaginative, and all the more impressive for having been written by the pupil of a school that a large proportion of the town liked to pretend didn't exist. In sending the story to the paper, Mr Thomas had thought he would be doing a service both to St Jude's and Adam himself. In the end, however, it was a case of 'the good news and the bad news'. The good news was that Adam did win the competition. It was published in the paper alongside a photograph of himself and his classmates. Subsequently, other 'Animal Tales' that he put together were also published. The bad news was that the high quality of the story unleashed a storm of recriminations and counter-recriminations about the very existence of the school. Having drawn attention to their star pupil, St

Jude's suddenly found themselves confronted with the prospect of closure.

Thankfully, the children remained largely ignorant of all these goings-on and life continued at St Jude's much as before.

For Adam, once he was well again, this meant continuing his search for the reason why he was able to communicate through Mammalogue. Strangely enough, it was in a religious studies lesson some months later that he suddenly felt he might be getting close.

As there was a complete range of religions represented at the school, a wide variety of festivals, legends and leaders were looked at. Occasionally, the parents would bring in special cakes or biscuits to celebrate one of the many holy days. While on special trips, they would visit churches, mosques, cathedrals and temples. Despite the almost bewildering diversity of traditions and beliefs the children were exposed to, however, there was one particular story which all of them seemed to know in some shape or form.

To Adam, who had spent so many afternoons playing with his Ark and listening to the distant voices of the animals it held, the old story was quite familiar – or at least the bare bones were. That weekend, all the children had to quiz their parents on the exact details of the story of the old man who had gathered the animals together to save them from the flood.

"Well, I'm not altogether sure of all the details," Miriam had said. "Hang on, let's look it up."

She'd found the reference in the Bible and read it through to herself.

"Right," she said, finally closing the book. "Well, when Noah was six hundred years old, God told him that as the men and women of the world were so wicked, he was going to destroy it all. Then he told Noah to build a huge Ark, three hundred cubits long."

"How long is a cubit?" Adam had asked.

"Oh, about this long," Miriam had answered, waving her arms about ambiguously. "Anyway, he built the Ark and then he and his wife, his sons and their wives went out and collected a male and a female from every species of animal, so that after the flood had subsided, they would all be able to re-populate the earth."

When Adam had finished listening to Ifham and Abdul's story on the Monday morning, he realized that the version they had in their Koran was almost identical. It was Chandra's turn next. Her parents came from India and she told them all a story that her mother remembered from a book called the *Bhagavata Purana*. At first the story started off strangely: about a devout old king called Satyavrata and a fish. But as she continued, it became increasingly familiar: the old king was given a warning to make preparations for a flood which God was sending because man was so bad. Satyavrata's task was to go out and call together a pair of animals from every species.

Having established that the tale existed in all their religions, the children set to, building their own Ark and making masks of the animals, so that they could act out the story.

Adam sat on his own in a corner quietly. Unanswerable puzzles were spinning round and round inside his head.

He'd never really given it much thought before but, how had Noah managed to call all the animals together? And how had they all agreed on a truce not to harm or even eat each other during their year-long voyage? There could be only one answer.

Mammalogue.

All of a sudden, everything seemed to fall into place. *He* could talk to animals, couldn't he? Did that mean that a new flood was coming? Or something worse? Something that

95

would wipe out the entire animal population of the world? Was *he* destined to be the new Noah?

"It can't be true," he muttered to himself nervously. "It can't be!"

But what other reason could there be for his being able to speak to the animals?

He was just a boy. One single, solitary, almost-eleven-year-old. What could *he* do? he wondered, as his panic grew. Clamping his hands over his ears, he hoped that for once he would hear silence. If only all the distant noises would go away. But there, as always, was the far-off sound of constant murmurings.

'What do you want me to do?' Adam asked desperately.

There was no reply.

As a climax to the whole Ark project, it was announced that the following Friday they would all be going to the zoo. Adam was beside himself with excitement. It was somewhere his mother had been promising to take him for so long, but whenever they had the day planned, something or other would go wrong. Once, the car refused to start. Another time they got half-way there when a van crashed into the side of them and they had to drive back home. Or it rained. Or Adam got ill. There always seemed to be some excuse.

But on that bright, blustery morning in April, nothing went wrong. The children assembled in the school playground at seven and by half-past they were speeding off towards their destination singing, almost appropriately, 'Old MacDonald Had a Farm'!

—9—
THE ELEPHANT'S MEMORY

'So how was it?' Oscar asked finally.

'I thought you were never going to ask,' Adam thought back.

'I wasn't.'

Although she had heard Adam get back from his trip all loud and full of the day's events some hours earlier, she had remained obstinately hidden at the top of the airing-cupboard.

If he wants to tell me, he'll have to come and find me, she had thought disdainfully.

In the event the boy hadn't bothered. He'd prattled on and on to Miriam about everything he'd seen and evidently hadn't spared a thought to his most loyal companion. She listened closely to what he was saying, but from her place of concealment, she could only hear the words he was exceptionally excited about.

". . . brown bears . . . pandas . . . sweeeeet . . . tiny . . . tigers . . ."

Sitting there, growing increasingly frustrated and angry, she finally decided she might as well make an appearance. And leaping down on to the lino, she padded through the bathroom and down the stairs to the kitchen. Tail high, nose in the air, she marched past them haughtily, straight to her food bowl. It would have had more effect if she could have been able to nibble fastidiously at food they had put down for her, but Adam's arrival home had apparently made Miriam forget all about the cat's feeding-time.

She continued walking and stepped angrily through the cat-flap and out on to the patio. She was blowed if she'd ask how he was.

Yes, Oscar was jealous – and she wasn't afraid to admit it.

All those years she had spent dedicating her life to the well-being of the boy and now he was prepared to just go gallivanting off to zoos and consort with all manner of exotic intruders. Of course, she had always known that the day would come when he was an adventurous little boy and she was a tired elderly lady. But that didn't make the changes any easier to bear. She was being usurped and she didn't like it. It wasn't fair.

She sat out on the lawn, watching the sparrows hopping around from tree to path and back again, totally unconcerned by the presence of the cat. Did she really look that old and harmless now? she wondered. The equivalent of sixty-five human years, she knew that she was slower than she used to be. But there was life in the old girl yet.

Her tail twitched angrily and her eyes narrowed as she twisted herself round into a position ready to pounce.

Cheeky little so-and-so's, she thought, as the sparrows bounced around inches away from her paws. I may be older, but my claws are still sharp enough to teach you a lesson. And she rolled her shoulders and poised herself, ready to strike. The sparrows merely continued to peck away at seeds in the grass.

Geronimo!

Oscar launched herself off into the air. Just as agile as ever! she thought proudly, and landed with her paws squarely over one of the insolent little birds. 'Gotcha!'

Taking care not to let her prey escape, she lifted one paw off the grass. Nothing. The sparrow must have twisted round under her chest. She raised the other paw. Still nothing. She leapt to her feet and danced around, looking for the sparrow that she *knew* she had caught – but it was nowhere to be seen. The sound of twittering from the top of the fence behind her increased. Oscar interpreted the sound as mocking laughter. There was simply no denying the fact that time was slipping away.

She noticed the light in Adam's room going on. The boy was still so young – he had the whole of his life to look forward to, while she was already past it. Oscar realized that she was stupid being so pompous and dismissive about his trip to the zoo. Hadn't she herself warned Adam that she wouldn't be around for ever and that he ought to prepare himself for that day? That was all he was doing.

Swallowing her pride, she trotted back through the cat-flap and up the stairs to his bedroom.

'I'm sorry,' she thought.

Adam gave the cat a big affectionate cuddle.

'Already forgotten,' he thought back. 'Now, do you want to hear about the zoo or not?'

'Go on then.'

And as his story of the day began to unfold, Oscar felt even more guilty about not being there when Adam had arrived home, to hear what had happened. It soon became clear that the boy's initial wonder had rapidly turned to sadness and bewilderment. The trip to the zoo had raised far more questions than it had answered, and far from discovering the purpose of Mammalogue, Adam had almost come to the conclusion that his ability to talk to the animals was a curse rather than a gift.

In the coach that morning, Adam had known how near they were getting to the zoo without needing to look at the road-signs. All he had to do was close his eyes and listen to the approaching babble of a thousand voices. The mounting excitement he felt at the prospect of meeting all the animals he'd so far only played with in his Ark and read about in the encyclopaedia was becoming unbearable. Surely here he'd be able to find out more about Mammalogue.

One by one, the stream of children passed through the clunking turnstiles. When Adam's turn came, he grinned happily as he entered the confines of the zoo.

'Hello, hello, HELLO,' he thought as loudly as he could to announce his arrival.

And while the rest of the class made a beeline for the gift-shop, Adam walked down the central path towards the animals. Slowly, reverently, as if he was walking down the aisle of a beautiful cathedral, he approached the enclosures.

Adam could hardly believe the cacophony of noise that was now filling his head. All those distant sounds and voices that he'd heard down the years were suddenly surrounding him, bewildering him, as each individual animal bellowed for his attention.

"But who should I visit first?' he muttered. "Which of the animals will be able to explain Mammalogue to me?"

He stopped and looked down the list of animals on the central signpost. The whole zoo had been divided up into sections which represented the continents. As Adam scanned the board, he realized there was only one choice.

It was in the wide land mass which is now called Africa that the mammals first emerged, and though they had spread to populate the world as the continents drifted apart, Africa today remains the heart of the mammalian population. Surely, Adam had reasoned, if there *was* an answer to the riddle of Mammalogue, it would be the animals of Africa who held the key.

Guided by the insistent trumpeting of the continent's largest mammal, Adam soon found his way to the right section of the zoo. And there, the first animal he was confronted by was the source of all the noise: the massive African elephant.

Despite all the photographs, films and videos Adam had seen before, faced with the gigantic, grey beasts standing in front of him, ears flapping, trunks swinging, feet trampling the ground and raising clouds of dust, Adam couldn't help gasping at their sheer enormity. He stood there staring at them: unable to think.

Unable to use Mammalogue.

In the end, it was one of the elephants who communicated first.

'So you finally decided to visit us,' the largest male thought to Adam.

The sound in his head was deeper than anything the boy had heard before. It was a bit like talking in an empty room – echoing and solemn.

'I *was* coming,' Adam thought back. 'I . . .'

'Well, you certainly took your time about meeting the most impressive mammal that ever walked the earth,' the elephant snorted.

'And the most modest?'

'Modesty be blowed. Just look at me,' it thought, and with its ears fully extended it tilted its head back, raised its trunk and trumpeted so loudly that the noise bounced all round the zoo. For a moment, every other squeak, chatter, grunt, growl and roar ceased.

'Hear the respect I command,' the elephant thought proudly.

Adam nodded. He looked around the enclosure: there were seven elephants in all, ranging from a tiny, hairy infant right up to the twelve-foot tall, twenty-five foot long, fifteen and a half thousand pound adult in front of him. If anyone knew about Mammalogue, it should be the elephants, he thought, and he proceeded to outline his reasons for wanting to come to the zoo so much.

'And so you're trying to find out *why* you have the gift of Mammalogue?' the elephant repeated. 'And you think that I – or we,' it added with a swing of its trunk, 'might have the answer.'

'Well, if the most important animal doesn't know, then I suppose none will,' Adam thought back flatteringly.

'Ah, but I said I was the most *impressive*, not the most *important*,' explained the elephant. 'There may be a difference. I think it's up to you to discover for yourself which animal you think to be the most important.'

'Can't you just tell me?'

'I can tell you what I know. No more, no less,' the elephant replied cryptically. 'Come round the other side, we won't be disturbed there.'

The elephants' enclosure was a raised circular area, surrounded by a deep moat that they couldn't cross. At the back, in the shade of a giant oak tree, the moat was slightly narrower, and it was here that the elephant told Adam to sit down, close his eyes and stretch his arm out. He did as he was told and felt his fingertips being lightly touched by the soft end of the elephant's extended trunk. Warm breath was blown gently into his palm. And as he felt his entire body gradually being enveloped by the elephant's warmth, the darkness behind his eyes was replaced with a new and wonderful landscape.

'This is where I was born,' he heard, and Adam realized that he was in the centre of the African savannah of the elephant's memory.

'It's beautiful.'

'My name, by the way, is Cana. Welcome to Africa.'

Having been brought up in the suburbs of a small town, the shock of finding himself in the centre of endless plains left Adam wordless. It was all so huge. Little wonder that animals as massive as the elephants had evolved. All round him, the gently rolling grassland sloped away towards distant horizons. The unending patchwork of green grass and red earth was broken only by the delicate acacias and solid baobab trees which dotted the landscape. And among them, looking almost like trees and bushes themselves, were the animals. In every direction he looked – thousands upon thousands of them. Giraffe and gazelle, lion and rhino, zebras and cheetahs, impala, hyena, wildebeest, waterbuck, warthogs and, of course, the largest of them all, the elephants; crossing over the plains in their great, grey lumbering herds.

But although everything was so new, so unfamiliar, so awe-inspiring, Adam was overcome with an inexplicable sensation of having arrived home. He looked up, and the patterns of clouds across the huge sky were like a reflection of the ground below. Tiny wisps of white and grey were scattered across the wide expanse like the trees and animals below them. It all felt so *right*.

'There is an old story: "The Myth of the Moon." Every animal knows it,' Cana thought to Adam. 'They say that in the beginning there was a blue sky above and a green and featureless earth below. At night, the moon gave off vapours which surrounded the earth in wonderful shaped clouds, and cast intricate shadows on the earth which took the forms of hills and valleys. And slowly, some of the clouds descended and took root in the new soil and became the trees and shrubs. Later, watching the clouds which had remained in the sky, these immobilized clouds began to regret that they'd sacrificed their freedom of movement and pulled themselves up by the roots. Destined never to rise back into the sky, however, they grew legs and wandered, as animals, over the plains. Even today, the skin of the rhinos and elephants is like the smooth, grey bark of the baobab.'

Adam continued to sit there silently. He had, of course, heard many myths and legends about the origins of the world. Noah's Ark, for instance. But it had never occurred to him that animals could have myths of their own.

'A lot of things don't seem to occur to humans,' Cana chided. 'But no more of that. You wanted to know which mammal was the most important, and I think I've found you the ideal guide. Look.'

A herd of elephants was making its way slowly across the plains, heading towards some distant water-hole. As it passed the little hillock where Adam was sitting, the youngest of the group detached itself from the rest and trotted over towards the boy.

'Hi,' he announced himself and stuck his stubby little trunk out for Adam to take hold of. 'Follow me.'

Adam got up obediently and the pair of them ran back down the hill to catch up with the rest of the herd. For what seemed like hours, they all walked along in a solemn procession under the burning sun, passing groups of grazing animals that would look up for a moment before returning to their grassy meal. The elephants themselves seemed to eat everything that grew. They would rip out huge tufts of grass, shake them and push them into their mouths; they would stop and strip a couple of bushes bare; passing an acacia, one paused a moment for a few mouthfuls of bark before continuing its walk; and a little later on, one of the largest elephants put its head down against a tree and uprooted it to get at a cluster of juicy fruit it hadn't been able to reach, even with its trunk fully extended.

The amount of vegetation a herd of hungry elephants could get through was phenomenal, Adam realized. Nothing made this more clear than their excitement on coming across a baobab tree. Now the baobab is enormous. Its trunk is so broad that ten men surrounding it could *just about* link hands. But to the frenzied elephants, it might have been a cardboard box. They reduced the magnificent old tree to wood pulp in a matter of minutes.

'But why did they have to do that?' Adam asked.

'Our diet,' the baby elephant explained. 'The baobabs have got certain essential minerals.'

'It's a pity you can't get vitamin pills out of a bottle like us,' Adam commented flippantly.

'*They* probably come from plants and trees originally as well,' one of the others retorted, turning round to him.

Adam reddened with embarrassment. The elephant could well be right.

'It just seems that an awful lot of vegetation is being destroyed,' he added quietly, so that only his young companion would hear.

'True,' he replied. 'But sometimes it's good to get rid of the old trees and make way for the new. Also, we get a lot of forest fires started by lightning. They burn out when they get to the areas we've cleared. What's more,' he continued, 'we clear tracks down to the water-holes. If it wasn't for us, the weaker, smaller animals would die of thirst. We're really quite useful,' he concluded.

'Perhaps the most important animal,' Adam thought back, wondering whether his search was already over.

'Well, humans can't believe that — otherwise they wouldn't be slaughtering so many of us,' the small elephant muttered bitterly.

'You mean for the ivory?' asked Adam. He had read how poachers killed thousands of elephants each year for their valuable tusks, which could be carved into statues, bangles and beads.

'That as well . . .' the elephant replied. 'You'll see.'

They had finally reached the water-hole, and the ones who had been at the front of the line were already splashing around, stirring up the mud, squirting jets of water over their backs and at each other, drinking their fill. Adam was struck by how gentle all of them were with one another. They communicated with deep, deep sounds that he could barely hear, but which evoked tender responses from the listener. And then, wrapping their trunks together, they would rough and tumble on the ground together, sending clouds of dust flying up into the air.

'But who else would want to slaughter you?' Adam asked.

'Shhh!' the baby elephant insisted.

In the distance, Adam noticed a rumbling sound. It was approaching. The elephants had heard it too and were turning this way, then that, splashing round in confused circles. The baby elephant automatically sought out his mother and pushed his trunk into her mouth for comfort. The noise was getting closer, and the elephants nervously left the water. One of them lifted its head and let out a bellowing trumpet which echoed back against the sky. As one, they all took off, trampling down the trees in their frantic effort to escape the advancing noise that they knew meant danger.

Above the sound of the engines now, they could hear raised voices. Instructions being shouted. And some of the trucks drove round to the far side to head the elephants off as they emerged from the undergrowth. Meanwhile, drowning out all other noise and whipping the dust, leaves and twigs up into a blinding fog, was a helicopter which had arrived out of nowhere and was now hovering overhead.

'What's happening?' Adam screamed, as he stood fixed to the spot while bedlam reigned all round him.

A moment later, the tiny elephant, now separated from his mother, bumped into him. Adam patted his rough, hairy back reassuringly.

'It'll be all right.'

'It won't, it won't,' the elephant muttered miserably. 'Listen.'

And as Adam strained to hear something above the throbbing beat of the helicopter blades, there was the unmistakable sound of gunfire.

'Noooo!' the baby elephant trumpeted and rushed off into the thick swirling dust.

With his T-shirt pulled up to shield his eyes, Adam made his way out of the thicket and into the clearing. The sight which he was confronted with when the dust had finally settled was like the scene from a great battle. The helicopter had landed and was standing like a giant dragonfly behind the trucks. There were twenty of them in all, and already the corpses of the elephants were being winched up on to them. If they had been poachers after the valuable ivory, Adam could at least have understood what was happening, but the words on the sides of all the vehicles made the massacre all the more terrible: African Department of Game.

"*Why?*" he screamed, as the men continued their job of loading the trucks with the dead elephants. If only he had known what was going to happen. Perhaps he could have stopped it. But now it was too late.

He looked around at the one survivor of the slaughter. It was the baby elephant, looking even smaller and more vulnerable than ever now. Standing next to the body of his dead mother, he was moaning quietly. A dismal, single note of despair that every so often would give way to a long, passionate bawl of misery. Refusing to believe that his mother could really be dead, he would kneel down next to her and try to nuzzle her back to life.

He was inconsolable.

When the last of the dead bodies had been cleared away, the men turned their attention to the baby elephant. They said something in a language which Adam couldn't understand and then shot a sedative dart into the elephant's rump. He looked around in panic for a couple of seconds, wobbled, staggered and then collapsed in a heap. When they were sure he was out for the count, the men rolled the unconscious animal on to a tarpaulin and hauled him up on to the one truck which remained empty. Remaining out of sight, Adam leapt up on to the back, and rode alongside the sleeping baby elephant.

Back at the camp, it soon became clear what they intended to do with their catch. A crate was swiftly prepared with straw and, as the drug slowly wore off, the drowsy elephant was pushed inside. The wooden door was slammed shut and securely locked. A man stapled an address label on to slats at the top and front and, having ensured that everything was ready, he joined the others in the canteen. Adam approached the crate and pushed his fingers through the gaps. Obviously frightened, though grateful for the little bit of contact, the elephant gripped Adam's fingertips with the end of his trunk and blew warm air down his arm.

Adam read the name and destination on the label.

"But you're . . ." he said and opened his eyes.

'Yes,' Cana replied, 'the little orphan. I was shipped here twenty years ago.'

Just to make sure, Adam looked around him. He was

back in the zoo, with his outstretched fingers still lightly touching the elephant's trunk. It had all been Cana's life story.

'But it was so horrible,' he thought, sighing. 'Why did they do it?'

'It's called culling,' the elephant explained. 'They said there were so many of us we were destroying the environment and that was their so-called *scientific* solution.'

'Well . . .' Adam started to say, remembering the state of the baobab tree.

'Would you like to hear a couple of real scientific facts?' Cana interrupted. 'The population of the local *people*, not the elephants, is doubling every twenty-five years. Human farmers, not elephants, are destroying natural plant cover and turning the land into desert: the Sahara is now advancing at a rate of fifty miles per year. Forty-five years ago seventy per cent of East Africa was occupied by elephants, now we're only allowed on seventeen per cent of the land in isolated game parks. In the area you call Sudan, 548 million acacia shrubs are pulled up every year – not by elephants, but by humans who like their food cooked. But then human scientists know all this as well as I do,' he added and snorted, 'yet they still prefer to cull us instead.'

Adam looked down at his feet. Cana's criticisms about scientists were making him feel increasingly ill at ease. He thought of his father and his work at Dimwell's Research Institute. What exactly *did* he do there? He was beginning to suspect that the answer to Mammalogue might lie there, rather than in the zoo.

'And it won't work,' Cana was continuing. 'It can't work. When there's a food shortage, *we* have fewer calves – nature ensures we don't breed too many. But mankind! Not a clue. It's human ignorance of the fragile balance of everything around them which is so damaging. If they lower the number of elephants, another problem will inevitably arise.'

"The food-chain again," Adam muttered to himself, remembering both his nightmare and the row with his father.

'And the point is,' Cana continued, 'it's simply not possible for us to get far enough away from humans ever to live safely again. There are some six billion of you on earth while, at the last count, a few hundred thousand of us living in the wild. Did you know that poachers are now killing two thousand elephants *a week* for their tusks. Now, given those sorts of odds – well, I know where I would put my money. I guess African elephants are doomed to follow the mammoths and quaggas and dodos down the one-way street to extinction.'

'Oh, don't say that,' Adam pleaded. The elephant's story sounded so familiar; like the fox's tale, like the hedgehog's. Wherever Adam went, whatever animal he spoke to, the story was the same. And yet he couldn't allow himself to believe that there was no hope left.

'It's not over yet,' he thought. 'People can change.'

'But there isn't much time left, is there?'

'Oh, good grief, you're right,' Adam suddenly realized as he glanced at his watch. 'The coach is leaving in five minutes. I've got to go.'

'*I* don't know why you can speak Mammalogue,' the elephant added sadly, as Adam was hurriedly checking that he had everything. 'What makes a particular animal important? That's the question you've got to try and find an answer to.'

But Adam was only half-listening. If he got back to the coach late, he'd be in trouble.

'Bye!' he said.

'You *will* come back again, won't you?' Cana thought.

The sadness in the elephant's thoughts was unmistakable.

Adam realized with a jolt how insensitive he was being. It was all very well for him. He could simply leave the zoo now and return to his home – something the elephant and the other animals in the zoo would never be able to do.

The boy looked up into the dark eyes of the massive, gentle animal.

'Yes,' he said. 'I will be back. I promise.'

—10—
UNLUCKY THIRTEEN

On his thirteenth birthday, Adam woke up to the sight of a bicycle at the end of his bed. It was a brand-new, red, grey and shiny chrome, ten-speed racer. He'd asked for a skateboard and hadn't been sure his parents would even get him that. But a bike! He wouldn't even have dreamt of asking for one — his father was notoriously 'careful' with money, and since the showdown they'd had over Oscar's kittens, he had been particularly non-communicative. Perhaps the racing-bike signified a truce. Or perhaps it was to celebrate Adam's becoming a teenager. Or perhaps it was to compensate for the upheavals of the previous school-year which had been so fraught. Whatever the reason, Adam couldn't wait to try the bike out and he leapt out of bed and dressed himself in an instant.

He bumped it down the stairs and out through the front door.

"Be careful," he heard his mum calling and he turned round to wave.

Both she and his dad were standing there at the sitting-room window, watching him. Two familiar people. Both the same height: the one, big, with fair hair and brightly coloured clothes that never quite matched; the other, thin, pinched, in beige and grey. The unfamiliar aspect of the scene was that they were standing close together. He looked again. Yes, they were actually holding hands. It occurred to Adam that although they seemed so different that it was sometimes impossible for them to get on, they must still love each other. If only a little bit.

Adam set off, clicked the gears into an easier action and pedalled down the road opposite. He turned round to wave goodbye. His parents were both still standing there. Miriam waved back enthusiastically. Derek's attempt to see him off was altogether more awkward. The older Adam got, the sorrier he felt for his father – he was always involved in his work, he had no friends and was hopeless at dealing with his family. In his own way, he had as many difficulties communicating with others as Adam.

In fact, he was worse off.

Adam had Oscar.

The feeling of speed was something he'd always liked and that was exactly what the bike gave him. Fresh air in his face, wind in his hair, objects whizzing past, blurring across his vision. It was fantastic! But the best thing about the new bike was the independence it gave him. He would now be able to visit the zoo again. Something which the wrangles and recriminations of the previous year at school had prevented him from doing.

'Soon,' he thought out loud to the animals. 'I haven't abandoned you,' he added, feeling particularly guilty that Cana the elephant might think he had deliberately not kept his word.

The school outing to the zoo had provided Adam with the most wonderful day he had ever had — as well as the most disturbing. The moment he'd got back to the coach he'd pestered the three teachers mercilessly, until they had all solemnly promised that a follow-up trip would be arranged 'as soon as possible'. Satisfied that he'd done all he could to ensure he'd be back talking to the elephants, lions and all the others before too long, he'd joined in with the others singing 'Ten Green Bottles', 'London's Burning' and 'Yellow Submarine'.

In the event, all the plans and promises made that day went completely awry. A storm which had been brewing in the local education office over the previous year suddenly broke with a fury which took everyone by surprise. Teachers were accused of acting like prison warders. Education officers were deemed unfit to carry on with their profession. Parents divided themselves equally between the two warring factions: some felt sure that their children had benefited from being at a Special School; others were convinced their children would do better if now allowed to attend an ordinary school. The local press had a field-day, reporting each new twist and turn in the seemingly endless saga of St Jude's. While all this was going on Adam, who had unwittingly caused the whole furore, found himself the centre of a huge controversy. He was splashed across the pages of the papers, interviewed on community radio and television, and became the focus of a full-page spread in a national Sunday supplement.

And the cause for all this vitriolic back-biting? 'The Fox and the Fleas Who Outstayed Their Welcome', the story which Adam had written after saving Oscar from the wild fox. Mr Thomas, who had initially given the boy's tale so much exposure by sending it in to the short-story competition, had resigned in the hope that the disagreement would then die down. But it'd had the opposite effect and the row had snowballed throughout the winter and on into the spring term.

The basic arguments went like this.

One side, represented by the local councillors, ratepayers' action group and government education officers claimed that any child who could produce such an outstanding piece of work should not be in a Special School.

The other side, represented by the teachers, educational psychologists and board of governors countered that he had only been able to produce such an outstanding piece of work *because* of the school.

However, although none of the opponents of the school would actually come out and admit it, what they most resented was the fact that so much money was being spent on what they saw as an expensive luxury. They camouflaged these greedy reasons with talk of 'the childen's rights' and 'community care', but basically it all boiled down to one thing.

Money.

In the end a compromise was reached. All the children in the school would be re-examined, using a new IQ test. The top-scoring thirty-three per cent would be sent to ordinary local schools to complete their school days in a more integrated environment, while the rest of the children would remain in the smaller St Jude's. Neither side was particularly happy with the outcome, but no one could come up with a better alternative.

The conversation that followed the publication of the exam results between Miriam Williams and the education officer was the exact reverse of the one she'd had with his predecessor some seven years earlier. Once again, although she *knew* she understood her son best, her opinion didn't seem to carry as much weight as it should.

"And the improvement has been so astonishingly marked," the education officer stated, "that we really do feel that it would now be in the boy's best interest to attend the local school."

"But he still has enormous problems coping with children," Miriam countered. "They mimic the way he speaks, and he simply retreats into himself."

"I can fully sympathize with the problem, believe me," the education officer said, nodding benevolently, "but, you see, he's not going to be able to remain in a Special School for ever, is he? There is no, shall we say, *special society* he can enter. No, we sincerely feel that it is time for Adam to integrate himself into an ordinary school. His current needs are social, clearly not academic," he added, patting the result sheet. "It is a credit to St Jude's that he has come such a long way, but now he must learn to mix with other people. And Willowfields really is an excellent school. Wonderful headteacher. Superb teacher–pupil relationship."

Miriam realized that she had been beaten all over again. However much they pretended to listen to her arguments, they never had the slightest intention of giving any ground once their minds were made up.

"And if the school turns out to be completely inappropriate . . ."

"His social progress will be monitored and continually assessed," the education officer assured her. "There is really nothing for you to concern yourself about."

Although she sensed that Adam was upset by the news that he would have to move school, she had to admit that externally, at least, there was very little sign that leaving St Jude's bothered him. He'd shrugged and nodded, and asked whether they could have toffee ice-cream for pudding. She knew that if he was concerned it would be Oscar, not her, who would share his worries. And indeed, when the cat had returned for something to eat later that evening, Adam had waited for her to lick her food bowl clean before going upstairs with her. They had sat together for hours.

'What happens if I really hate it?'

'I don't think you will.'

'But you know how the local kids take the mickey out of me,' he thought back. 'I don't know. I can hear all the words OK in my head, but when I try to say them . . .'

'Oh, they'll hardly even notice,' Oscar thought encouragingly.

But Adam wasn't so sure. He'd watched the groups of children over in the park and in the bus station. He knew the way they spotted the slightest defect and ridiculed it non-stop. One girl had freckles and the others kept yelling that she'd got dog mess on her face. Another was fat and they'd simply grunted and snorted like pigs every time she'd tried to talk to them. While a boy suffering from a mass of acne on his face and neck was tormented by the group running round with their hands pressed against the sides of their heads shouting, "Squish that zit, squish that zit!"

The aim of all the taunting was to reduce the chosen victim to tears. And with none of them did it work better than the young boy who produced a 'w' every time he aimed for an 'r'. Time after time, Adam had seen him bawling his eyes out while the others circled round him; laughing, ridiculing.

"Whadda madda Wobert? Why ya cwying?"

"Ya vewy angwy?"

"Or misewable?"

"We're weally, weally, weally sowy fow upsetting ya."

"Pwomise!"

And they would all burst out laughing again.

'I know,' Oscar thought. 'Children can be extremely cruel to one another.'

'Unlike animals.'

'Oh, I don't know. I doubt whether anyone will *eat* you!' Adam laughed.

'Anyway,' Oscar continued, 'the difference between the spotty, fat, freckled Woberts of this world and you, is that *they* want to belong. You've got enough going for you to rise above all that.'

'How do you mean?' Adam asked.

'Do I really need to spell it out?' Oscar asked. 'You've got Mammalogue – it doesn't matter what they think of you in the end. You've got millions of friends, and nothing they can do or say can ever take that away from you!'

And whenever Adam started to feel uneasy about the prospect of starting at Willowfields in September, he hugged those words of comfort to himself like a baby's blanket. Oscar was right, just as she always was.

And so, a teenager at last, Adam was aware that his whole life was about to change. Not only was he about to start at Willowfield Comp.; not only was he the proud owner of a brand-new racing-bike, but he also felt confident that he was about to find the answer to the question that had been haunting him for so many years. Since he could now get to the zoo whenever he wanted, he'd surely discover precisely why he'd been born able to speak to animals. He would finally understand Mammalogue. It was a prospect so exciting, that Adam began pedalling all the faster.

Having cycled right round the road ringing the pedestrian zone, Adam headed back home again. He tried out all the gears: his legs labouring one moment, then spinning effortlessly round the next. The bike was brilliant. And he started making plans for his trips to the zoo. It was more of an uphill journey, but even taking that into account, it shouldn't take him too long to get there. And coming back would be a piece of cake.

There was just one accessory that the bike lacked, he decided as he turned back into his road. And that was a rack that he could attach Oscar's basket to. He knew that the cat would love going out for rides with him. Perhaps she'd even like to come to the zoo.

"Os!" he called as he pedalled up the alley and left the bike leaning against the garage. "Os—car! Where are you?"

The cat didn't appear, but Adam didn't give it much thought. The older she got, the more independent and cranky she was becoming. And today, being Adam's thirteenth birthday, meant that Oscar had reached the age of sixty-six and a half – although there was nothing in her behaviour to suggest she was prepared to slip into retirement just yet.

When Oscar still hadn't turned up by half past six, Adam was beginning to get just the slightest bit agitated. It was unusual for the cat to stay out all day and as it was his birthday, he'd have expected her to have come back earlier rather than later.

"Perhaps she's off visiting her boyfriends," said Miriam.

It was something she used to say when Adam was younger. It would make him laugh then, but now it just irritated him. She *knew* that since the incident with the fox, Oscar had had nothing to do with any toms. Why didn't parents notice their children outgrowing jokes?

"I'll go, look for her," Adam said.

"Have some tea first."

"Not hungry."

"Are you taking your bike?"

"Natch," Adam said with a grin.

"Well, take your lights."

"Not dark for ages. See you later," he shouted back, as he sped off down the road.

A couple of times she'd got stuck up trees in the park at the back, and although this time he couldn't hear her calling for help, he thought he'd try there first.

Being the first really warm evening they'd had that summer, the park was fuller than Adam had seen it all year. There were boys playing 'three and in' around one of the goal-mouths, a group of young girls playing French cricket, kids jumping across the stream, climbing over the tree trunks, cycling up and down the central hill on their BMXs. As always, the sight of so many children all together filled Adam with dread – as well as a slight resentment that they had all come over to *his* park because it was a bit warmer than usual. On the other hand, being on the bike made him feel that little bit more confident than usual.

Where to look? he wondered.

Going on previous experience, he cycled slowly along the path which ran through the woods by the stream, calling out for Oscar as he went. There was no response however, and he decided to head over to the wild area on the far side. Many years ago it had been the orchard belonging to a huge house. But the house had been destroyed in a fire and the fruit trees had all been left to go wild. Oscar claimed that the mousing and birding was exceptionally good there, and Adam had once had to rescue her from the top of a pear tree where he'd found her mewing pathetically.

She was not there today however. Nor up an apple, a cherry, a chestnut or any other sort of tree. What was more, though Adam closed his eyes and listened hard for the cat, he could only hear the distant sounds of countless animals. Oscar's was not among them. Or if it was, then it was too far away to be discernible. Adam was fairly convinced that the cat wasn't in the park at all.

Perhaps she's back home by now, he thought to himself, and he set off across the bumpy grass towards the park gates. He hadn't got half-way there when he heard a fearsome noise to his right. He glanced round and noticed a massive dog, its teeth bared, racing across the grass. For a moment, he thought he must be mistaken, but no, there was no doubt — it was heading straight for him. As it got closer, the snarling and barking became more frenzied and he could see streams of saliva hanging from its yellowed teeth. From somewhere in the distance, he could hear a boy's voice yelling, "Get him, Vic. Kill!" followed by the sound of raucous laughter.

Adam braked and looked back at the dog. It looked as if it was on the point of going for his throat.

'Calm down,' he instructed it.

The effect was instantaneous. The dog stopped, as if it too had suddenly applied the brakes, and stared up at the boy with its head cocked to one side and its tongue lolling comically out of the side of its mouth. The two words had effectively disarmed the dog, turning a slavering attacker into a clown.

'How do you do that?' the dog thought back.

'I just can,' Adam replied, laying the bike down on the grass. He then crouched down next to the dog and stroked it. 'You're a beautiful dog, aren't you?'

It wagged its tail appreciatively.

'So what was all that nonsense about?' Adam asked.

'The attack?' it thought, looking as sheepish as a dog can. 'I wouldn't have actually bitten you or anything, just frightened you a bit. I think the plan was to make you fall off your bike. It was *his* idea, anyway,' it added, nodding back behind it.

Adam looked up to see five kids of around his age racing up to where he was sitting on the grass, tickling the dog's stomach.

"Vic!" the tallest one yelled. "What do you think you're doing?"

Vic rolled over reluctantly.

"Heel, Vic!" he shouted. "Heel!"

The dog dragged himself up to his feet in a half-hearted attempt to obey. But just to show what he thought of the whole situation, he licked Adam in the face before loping off to his master's side.

"Never seen him do that before, Terry," said one of the girls in the group.

"Shut up!" Terry said. "And what's your name?" he asked, turning on Adam. "Wingnut?"

The others laughed.

"Eh, Wingnut?" he repeated, pulling at one of Adam's sticky-out ears. "'s gotta be."

"Adam."

"Adam what?" one of the others asked.

"Williams," he said. But even with that one word, he knew that the three boys and two girls in front of him had noticed his difficulty with certain sounds.

"Wwwillll-yams, huh?" one of them repeated, and the others laughed again.

"Wwwwing-nut Wwwillll-yams!" Terry said, twisting his face round as he spoke.

Adam could feel himself growing angry. He tried to think of Oscar's encouraging words: that Mammalogue had given him enough for this sort of conflict not to mean anything. He had millions of friends in the world.

All very well in theory, he thought.

But at that moment, Vic looked up.

'Ignore them, they're not so bad when you get to know them.'

'I believe you,' Adam thought back.

'I mean it. I've got an idea,' he thought, 'let's have a bit of fun at their expense.'

"Oy, Wingnut!" Terry suddenly yelled. "Are you listening to me?"

"No, yes, I . . ."

'Tell them you were trying to guess their names,' Vic said.

Adam did so.

"So what are they, then?" one of the girls sneered.

"Well, your name is . . .'

'Denise."

". . . Denise, and yours," he added, leaving Denise with her mouth wide open, "is Naima."

"How did you know that?" they both demanded in unison.

He turned to the others.

'Dexter and Ian,' the dog told him.

'Which is which?' Adam asked in a panic.

'Dexter's the black one.'

"You're Dexter. And you're Ian," he said.

"I don't know how you did that, but well done. Hundred per cent right," said Dexter, giving a little round of applause.

The others joined in.

"Hang on!" Terry said, sensing that he was being upstaged. "Why's the dog called Vic?"

"Simple," said Adam, after a word in his ear from the dog in question. "Short for Vicious."

The ripple of applause went round the group again.

"So what're you doing in our park anyway?" Terry asked.

Adam thought he wouldn't tell them the main reason for

123

being there. He felt a bit guilty denying Oscar's existence like that, but well, he *was* a teenager now.

"Just trying out my new bike," he said.

"'s a bit flash," said Ian. "Let's have a go."

"I ought to be going," said Adam.

"Don't you trust me?" he asked, moving towards the bike.

Vic gave a warning growl.

"Here, what's got into that dog of yours?" Ian demanded.

"Search me," said Terry.

Adam used the moment to pick up the bike himself and set off.

"See you," he called back.

"See you," Naima and Denise called back.

"Oh, liked him, did ya?" Adam heard Terry saying to them, as he pedalled off towards the gates. "Liked our little wingnutted chum, eh?"

"How *did* he guess our names though?"

Adam's immediate thought was to get back home and tell Oscar how well he'd managed to deal with a situation with 'normal' kids. He wanted to tell the cat that despite all she'd said about dogs and how stupid they were, he'd met one who was really all right. But when he got back, it soon became clear that Oscar still hadn't returned.

"I just don't know where she is," Miriam said. "But I'm sure she's all right."

"But she's never out this late," Adam persisted. "Never, and she knows it's my birthday."

"Well, perhaps she's getting you something extra special," Miriam said, knowing that she was clutching at straws.

"Why don't you phone the police?" he demanded.

"Tomorrow," she said.

"Why not now?"

"It's getting dark and they'll . . ." she began.

A knock at the door interrupted her logical, albeit untruthful, explanation.

"It's her," Adam yelled, "and she's hurt!"

He was right. When Mrs Williams opened the door, she was confronted with a man carrying a very bedraggled cat. He explained how he had found her staggering along the road, dazed and muddled.

"I think he must have been hit by a car," he said. "Lucky he was wearing a name tag. Oscar, nice name."

"It's a 'she' actually," she said. "Oh, but thank you so much for bringing her back. My son was getting so ... Thank you."

He put the cat down in the hall and the three of them watched as she pulled herself up on to her legs and stood there wobbling unsteadily. Looking up and round, she finally located Adam and mewed plaintively.

'What happened?' Adam asked.

'Car,' Oscar confirmed. 'I'll never get used to which way I have to look first.'

'Look right, look left, look right again, if all clear ...' Adam began to recite.

'I know the words,' Oscar interrupted. 'It's my right and left I have problems with. Oh dear,' she added, 'I'm going to have to lie down for a while.'

And with that she attempted to trot off towards her basket in the kitchen. It was far from an easy journey. She zigzagged falteringly down the hallway, occasionally bumping into the walls as she did so. It was all Adam and Miriam could do to stop themselves bursting into laughter at the cat who looked, for all the world, as though she was completely drunk.

''snot funny,' she muttered with as much dignity as she could muster, before disappearing through the door.

Later that evening, when Oscar was beginning to get

back to normal again, Adam apologized for being so insensitive.

'That's all right, I must have looked fairly stupid,' Oscar thought back.

'You looked as if you'd been at Dad's whisky,' Adam replied. 'I knew you'd be all right anyway. It was only your eighth life after all.'

'My eighth, eh?' Oscar commented. 'I'm going to have to be extra careful from now on then, aren't I?'

—11—
LOCAL KIDS

'Facts and figures aren't worth the time it takes to work them out unless they're used properly,' Oscar had thought to Adam as he came to the end of yet another depressing tale told to him by one of the zoo animals.

Ever since he'd got his bike, Adam had used every opportunity to cycle the thirty miles to the zoo to learn more about the mammals there. The disappointment that he'd felt when the elephant wasn't able to tell him what Mammalogue might be for had soon faded away. What remained were the memories of that short walk through the African savannah. They persisted so strongly that he had known he would have to go back. Even if he never found the answer he was looking for there. Even if Dimwell's rather than the zoo held the key to the enigma. Even if there *was* no answer to Mammalogue, he realized that he was in such a unique situation to understand animals that he couldn't pass it up.

Some day it would come in useful.

He'd originally intended taking Oscar with him, but in the end it had proved impossible to persuade her.

'You go without me,' she insisted. 'I don't much like the sound of all those wild animals.'

'But we agreed to go together,' Adam had protested.

'They probably wouldn't even let me in anyway,' she added.

This was a possibility that Adam hadn't even considered. The more he thought about it, however, the more likely it seemed. After all, they had prairie dogs, lizards and baby penguins living in outside enclosures – even though he was loathe to admit it, he wouldn't like to guarantee that Oscar could last the whole visit without having a go at them. The temptation would be far too great and in the end, having promised that he'd recount every detail to the invalid on his return, Adam set off alone.

Ironically, it was now the faithful recounting of those details that was causing problems between them.

Every time Adam cycled to the zoo, he would come back with more sorry tales. And every time he related those tales, Oscar would get at him. It seemed to Adam that she was quite simply getting too old to be bothered.

'Well, does that mean he was right or wrong?' the boy asked.

'Oh, I'm sure everything he said was correct, but *so what*, unless it's actually used for a good purpose.'

Adam fell into a sulky silence. Even since her accident with the car, she'd been getting more and more awkward. It wasn't his fault that the stupid cat had been knocked down.

On his latest trip, he had learnt from a Siberian tiger that there were only some 150 of them living in the wild. Of the three in his litter, he was in captivity and his brother and sister were being worn by elegant ladies in Paris and New

York. Seeing that they were all in the same family, Adam had thought that the cat might be interested.

He'd evidently totally misjudged her.

'Well, Tom said . . .' Adam started.

'Tom, Tom, Tom,' the cat taunted. 'That's all I ever hear from you these days.'

All the employees at the zoo had got to hear about the boy who cycled thirty miles to be with the animals whenever he had the chance, but it was Tom Hutchinson whom Adam had got to know best. He was a Senior Keeper at the zoo and had been working there since he was a teenager — some twenty-odd years in all. It was the hyenas they had to thank for their initial meeting.

Still trying to find out the meaning of Mammalogue, Adam had taken a *memory-trip* back to the African savannah with Roc and Cuta, the two zoo hyenas. This was against his better judgement as he'd instinctively mistrusted the two loping, giggling, snarling animals. And he had been right not to trust them, for the moment they got on to the plains, they had abandoned the boy. Hour after hour Adam had trudged around under the scorching African sun, terrified that he'd never find his way back. When the hyenas finally did return, sniggering at his terror, Adam was totally exhausted. On finding himself back in the zoo, he had collapsed.

When he came round, he had looked up and found himself staring into a different pair of eyes. Not the scornful, brown animal eyes he last remembered seeing. These were blue and obviously concerned.

"Are you all right, son?" the man asked.

"Yes," Adam said uncertainly. "What happened?"

"You must have fainted," he explained. "Someone found you lying over there, next to the hyenas' cage."

"You're a keeper," Adam said, noticing the man's peaked cap and green uniform.

"I am, Tom Hutchinson's the name," he said, placing the boy down on a bench. "I know who you are too."

Adam suddenly felt worried. Could he have found out about the trips he went on with the animals of the zoo? Was he going to get told off?

"You're the boy that cycles over here, aren't you?" he continued. "Heard a lot about you. You must love animals."

"I do," said Adam, nodding.

"Well, look," he said, "I'm not free just yet, but at five o'clock I'll run you and your bike back home in the van."

"Oh no, it's . . ."

"Don't argue. You're in no fit state to ride at the moment."

And he had done just that: driven boy and bike back home. Miriam and Derek had been relieved to find that there was someone at the zoo who was at hand in case of emergency. Miriam, in particular, had been unhappy about the distance Adam had to cycle, although she would never have said anything.

Oscar was a different proposition altogether. From the first mention of the keeper, she had gone all huffy and distanced. She was clearly jealous. Tom was further proof — as if she needed any — that Adam was growing up and would soon have no further use for his old pet cat.

Adam realized that he had offended Oscar once again by mentioning the zoo-keeper. He hadn't done it deliberately, but Oscar was so touchy these days.

'Well, what do you think I should do about it then?' he asked.

'Search me,' Oscar replied peevishly. 'You're the bright young thing with all the energy. I'm too old and jaded and cynical to make any worthwhile suggestions.'

Adam looked away, hurt.

'You still haven't discovered exactly why you can speak

Mammalogue, have you?' she added, a little more softly.

Adam shook his head, miserably.

'Well, there must be a reason. If you'd just find that out . . .'

'Don't you think I've been trying?' Adam snapped angrily, and it was Oscar's turn to be offended.

Adam turned away and looked out of the window irritably. Over the last few months Oscar had been getting on his nerves more and more. Perhaps it was because she was always there – since the car crash she'd been increasingly reluctant to leave the house. Or maybe he was losing patience with the way she was becoming so niggly and grumpy in her old age. The only other possibility was that Adam, rather than Oscar, was changing.

Ever since he'd lied to the kids in the park about what he was doing there, he realized he was becoming embarrassed by his friendship with a cat. And as his voice had deepened and fine, downy hairs had started growing above his upper lip, he'd begun to find the cat increasingly childish. Even Mammalogue hadn't disguised the fact that they were growing apart.

'It's pointless to keep going to the zoo,' he continued sullenly. 'Anyway, my bike's got a puncture.'

'Well, you can mend it, can't you?'

'Of course I can mend it,' Adam scowled, 'I'm not an idiot.'

'I never said you were.'

'I'm sick and tired of Mammalogue,' he continued. 'It's because of this stupid language that everyone's treated me like a half-wit all my life. Special schools, Dad losing his temper the whole time: and I *still* don't sound quite right when I speak. It's not fair. I just want to be normal. Boring and ordinary and a hundred per cent normal.'

'You'd . . .'

'I don't want to listen to you or talk to you – or any of

the other animals in my head. I'm fed up with the constant jabbering.'

'You're upset,' Oscar thought comfortingly.

'I know I'm upset,' Adam thought back furiously. 'I've got this useless ability that doesn't benefit me or animals, or anything else for that matter. It just spoils everything. What's the point of me knowing how unpleasant human beings can be to animals? Huh? *I* can't do anything about it.'

Oscar stared hard at Adam. The teenager he'd become was so unlike the boy she'd grown up with. Obviously, she could understand his wish to fit in with his contemporaries, particularly now he was about to go to the local comprehensive. But she couldn't believe that his ability to use Mammalogue was pure chance. There *had* to be a reason for it.

'Perhaps you're not looking in the right place,' she suggested.

'What's that supposed to mean?' Adam shouted.

'Nothing,' Oscar thought back.

The boy was clearly in no mood to argue logically. Oscar decided to leave things well alone for the time being.

'Nothing? Then why say anything at all?' Adam persisted. 'Oh, damn it! I'm going over the park,' he announced.

'With some gang of young hooligans, I presume,' the cat sniffed dismissively.

'What would you know?' Adam snapped and left the room without waiting for a reply.

He'd arranged to meet the group of kids the day before. It had all happened because of the puncture he'd got on the way back from the zoo. Luckily, he was less than a mile away from home when it had happened. Cursing his luck, he'd dismounted and, keeping the flat tyre off the ground, had walked the rest of the way along the pavement. He had just been passing the church when someone called out.

132

"Oy!"

Assuming that it hadn't been intended for him, he kept walking. It was a horrible feeling when you turned round, only to find out that the person had been shouting to someone completely different.

"Oy, Wingnut!"

The addition of the nickname made it clear that someone *was* shouting at him. He turned round. Terry and Dexter were standing in the graveyard, waving their arms at him.

"Come over 'ere."

"I can't. I'm already late."

"Oh, come on. It's Vic."

Adam propped his bike up against the wall and went in. The pair of them were crouched down over a hole at the far side.

"Come out," Terry was shouting. "Vic!"

The dog had apparently caught sight or smell of an animal as they'd been walking past the cemetery and had dashed in after it. Whatever it was had bolted towards the hole and concealed itself inside. Too stupid and eager to realize that he'd get stuck, Vic had followed it. There was a faint sound of whimpering emerging from the blackness.

"Vic! Come out!" Terry yelled again.

Adam crouched down and listened carefully.

'Oh, help. Now what? I'm never going to get out now. And it's useless you keep shouting at me.'

'Vic.'

'Adam?'

'Yeah. What's happened?'

'I chased this cat down the hole and now I'm stuck.'

'Well, don't panic,' Adam thought back. 'If you could get in there, then you must be able to get out again.'

'I'm not so sure.'

The dog was obviously nervous, trapped underground in the black, airless tunnel.

133

"What's going on?" Terry asked.

"He's stuck."

"You what? Oh, no!"

"It's all right," Adam said.

"I'll go and phone the fire brigade, shall I?" asked Dexter.

"Hang on a minute," said Terry. He was watching Adam staring down into the hole, nodding occasionally, smiling, frowning: it looked just as if he was having a wordless conversation.

'You've got to get down really low, and then slide your back legs behind you and push with the front ones. That's it.'

'They're slipping.'

'Dig in with your claws.'

'I feel such an idiot.'

'I'm sure you look one too. You should never have gone into somewhere as narrow — you need cats' whiskers.'

'Don't talk to me about cats. I wouldn't be here now . . . ooh, this is tiring.'

'You're almost there,' Adam thought back encouragingly. He reached down inside the hole and felt for the dog's paw.

"My arm's not long enough," said Adam, "you try."

Terry thrust his arm in as far as he could get it.

"I can just feel something," he said.

'One more push,' Adam instructed the dog.

"That's it," said Terry.

"Pull very gently," said Adam, "otherwise you're going to dislocate his leg."

On emerging into the sunlight, Vic had gone crazy with happiness and relief, jumping all round the three of them, yelping and wagging his tail.

"Stupid dog," said Terry affectionately, playing with his ears and letting himself be covered with big wet licks. "I don't know how you did that," he said, turning to Adam, "but, well, cheers. Do you wanna come over the Pav? I'll get you a Coke or something."

"No, I really have got to get home," said Adam.

"Well, tomorrow then. Over the park."

"All right," said Adam, deliberately casual. "See you then."

Terry bent down to the dog again and noticed the scratches across his nose. "Hey, Vic, did that bad old fox cut you up a bit then?"

"It was a cat actually," Adam called back from the gate.

"How d'you know?"

"Vic er ... oh, it doesn't matter," he said, and left Dexter and Terry looking at the dog, at one another, at Adam, back at the dog; neither of them knowing what was going on.

And so, having argued with Oscar, Adam was stomping out of the house to go and find Terry and the others over the park. Before he'd even left the garden, he knew how unfair he'd been to the cat. It wasn't her fault he couldn't find out why he could speak to animals. The ironic side of it all was that whereas Mammalogue had prevented him from communicating with humans as a young boy, now it was doing the opposite. If he hadn't been able to think-speak to Vic, he'd never have got to know the other kids.

"Hey, Winger," he heard as he emerged from the woods.

The five of them were sitting on the bank of the stream while the dog splashed around in the water, apparently none the worse for the traumatic episode in the tunnel. As he walked over towards them, they all seemed genuinely pleased to see him.

"It's Winger Williams," said Terry.

"Hiya, Adam," Naima and Denise said in unison.

Adam looked from one to the other and nodded his hellos. And as he sat down, it occurred to him that he felt more at ease and comfortable with them than he'd ever felt with other kids before.

"Have a swig of this," said Terry, passing him a can. "This boy saved my dog yesterday," he said, turning to the others. "I don't know how he did it, but he definitely did."

"We know," said Denise.

"You've told us half a dozen times," said Ian.

"All right, all right," said Terry. He threw a couple of stones into the stream. "So, how *did* you do it?" he asked, turning back to Adam.

"What?"

"Get the dog out like that? It looked as though you were talking to him, almost."

"Oh, I'm just quite good with animals, that's all," said Adam. "I kind of thought encouraging thoughts to him."

Terry clearly wasn't convinced, but Naima butted in.

"It's like my gran," she said. "She had this mongoose back in Bombay."

"You're Indian?"

"Well, I was born here, but my family still live over there. Anyway, Gran's mongoose was almost human. It used to run up and down her arm, sit on her shoulder when she was reading. We all swore that they could talk to one another. And yet you should have seen it with a snake. I once saw it killing an enormous cobra."

"Same as my mum and her budgie," added Denise. "Horrible bird, but she gets it eating peanuts from her lips and everything. I come in some evenings and she's sitting there, watching the box with Bluey on her head."

Adam laughed. He was fairly sure that neither she nor Naima's grandmother could speak Mammalogue but, despite Terry's obvious interest, he didn't want to go into details.

"So which school are you at?" Ian asked.

Adam felt himself getting embarrassed again. Remembering how the local kids had always jeered as the school bus had gone past, he didn't want to have to say St Jude's.

"Oh, I'm just about to move to a new school," he said.

"Which one's that?"

"Willowfields. I start in September."

"Hey," they all yelled. "That's where we go."

"You'll hate it," said Dexter. "It's a pit."

"It's not that bad," said Ian.

"Unless he gets put in Tucker's class."

"How old are you?"

"Thirteen."

"No, he should go into Mrs Turnbull's, shouldn't he?"

"Or Mr Lingwood's."

Adam noticed with a sudden jolt of unease the way that Denise was staring at him. She had obviously recognized him but couldn't quite remember why. Presumably she'd seen his picture in the local paper – he'd been in it enough times, what with the stories and all the problems at St Jude's. He tried to ignore her and talk to the others as if nothing was up. But it was useless. He caught her eye again, and at that moment she suddenly realized exactly where she knew his face from.

Please don't say anything. Please don't! Adam thought desperately.

But Mammalogue only works with animals. Vic was looking at him curiously, wondering what was upsetting the boy, but Denise was totally oblivious to his pleas.

"You're the bloke that writes those animal stories, aren't you?" she said. "The one about the fox and the fleas. And the hedgehog and the tomatoes. And that sad one about the cat with the missing kittens. My mum reads them out to my younger brother. He loves them."

Adam looked down at the ground and nodded.

"What, we've got a writer in our midst, have we?" Ian said.

"Yeah," Denise continued, despite Adam's frantic wishing that she'd just stop. "You remember, all that stuff about St . . ."

It occurred to her why, instead of reacting positively to being recognized, the boy in front of her was furiously blushing to the tips of his sticky-out ears. She stopped.

"What was that, Den?" Naima asked.

"Nothing," she said, turning as red as Adam himself.

Terry had already clicked. He looked at Adam squirming around awkwardly. Ninety-nine times out of a hundred, he'd have had a field-day getting in his quota of laughs at someone else's expense. But there was something about the poor kid with the big ears and speech defect . . . Not that he was about to go soft. No, he owed it to him for rescuing his dog.

"St Jude's," he said. "Wasn't it?"

"What, the school for loonies?" Ian said.

Adam remained silent. He hated Mammalogue more than ever. Once again it was going to isolate him from other kids, keeping him locked in to his pointless communication with a whole load of miserable animals. He just wanted to be rid of it. But, as the encouraging thoughts coming from Vic confirmed, he couldn't shut it out. It would be like pretending to be blind or deaf. Mammalogue would not be denied.

"Oy, shut it!" Terry said, and the tone of his voice made it clear he was not joking.

"I only . . ." Ian protested.

"Well, don't only anything," he said. "I remember me dad talking about it. They kicked him out of the place, 'cause he was too clever, isn't that right? He's probably a lot cleverer than you too, dimbo," he added, pushing Ian on to his back.

"All right, Tel. Just a joke."

The atmosphere was becoming increasingly tense. Adam looked over at Terry. He didn't know how it had happened, but somehow he'd managed to win over an ally. Vic came splashing out of the water and licked Terry's face, giving his master a tacit seal of approval for the stand he'd taken. Then standing there, he shook all the water out of his shaggy coat, spraying the six children with dirty water.

"Hey, Vic," they all yelled, rolling away. "Clear off."

The atmosphere had been defused.

"Let's have a game of three 'n' in," Dexter said, standing up and dribbling the ball over towards the goal-posts. "Come on."

At first, Adam felt self-conscious about whether or not the others were going to laugh at him – the St Jude's football eleven had never been up to much – but before too long he was running around, passing the ball, heading and shooting with the rest of them. By the time it was getting dark, Adam had been in goal twice. And walking back home, he felt all sweaty and contented.

Humans might be cruel and thoughtless sometimes, but when they're on your side and like you, there's no nicer feeling than being accepted, Adam realized. But that didn't mean he could simply turn his back on all those who had been nice to him in the past.

'I'm sorry,' he and Oscar both thought at the same time when they saw each other.

'No, it was my fault,' they both went on, each trying to take the blame.

Adam burst out laughing.

I've been with this stupid animal so long, I'm even beginning to think like her, he thought. Or vice versa.

He bent down and, stroking the purring cat behind her ears, he told Oscar all about the so-called 'gang of hooligans'.

'Well, that was very commendable of them,' Oscar conceded, when Adam had finished. 'Particularly young Terry. And what do they all look like, these Good Samaritans? Just so that I might recognize them if *I* ever need a spot of help.'

'Well, Naima is thin with long black hair and her eyebrows meet in the middle. Her parents are from India. And Ian is about my height, but his hair is longer and a bit darker. And he kind of flicks it back like this,' he explained, tossing his head to one side. 'Dexter's black and his hair's cut so there's sort of two layers — short on the top and very short round the back and sides. And he's a bit taller than Ian. Then there's Denise. She's a bit fat. Not very, and she's always chewing gum. Her teeth are nice,' he added, remembering her smile. 'And Terry's the biggest. He's got thick, cropped hair, sticking up all over and . . . oh yes, this tooth here is chipped.'

'And the dog?'

'Vic's great,' he thought back enthusiastically. 'A kind of mixture of . . .'

'A mongrel,' the cat interrupted with a contemptuous sniff.

'Well, yes,' Adam had to admit. 'But a nice mixture. Shaggy hair, big, lopsided ears and his tail turns up at the end.'

'Sounds horrible.'

'Oscar! You're jealous!'

'Of a creature that doesn't know if it's a Dobermann or an Old English sheepdog. You are joking!'

"Adam!" Miriam called out. "Will you turn your light off now. It's late."

"All right, Mum," he called back.

And when he was in bed, he lay there thinking about the day he'd just had. Arguing with Oscar and wishing he couldn't communicate with animals. Then feeling so frightened that the other kids would pick on him. And in the end it had all been OK. If he could just balance the two, animals and humans, perhaps the new school wouldn't be so bad after all.

'Hey, Os. Os!'

He wanted to tell the cat that once again she had been right, but she was already breathing heavily in the basket beside his bed, fast asleep.

'Night, night, Oscar!' he thought.

—12—
WILLOWFIELDS COMP.

The first day at any new place can be difficult. And the night before Adam was due to start at Willowfields Comp., he lay in bed panicking. The fact that Oscar had assured him everything would be fine was suddenly irrelevant – *she* wouldn't be confronted with a sea of hostile faces in under twelve hours time. And the promise that Terry, Naima and the rest had made that he'd soon fit in wasn't any comfort either – *they* had already been there years and knew the ropes. However well he got on with all of them outside school, tomorrow he was going to have to face the situation on his own. It felt as if he'd been ordered to walk into a lion's den.

He closed his eyes and tried his best to forget all about the following morning. It would be a Monday, just like any other.

But it could be awful! a little voice whispered in his ear, and Adam began panicking all over again.

He felt scratchy and itchy, and even though his eyes were tired, his brain was wide awake. His only comfort was the distant murmur of the world of animals that he could hear inside his head. They were always there, the voices of the friends he'd made on his many trips when at the zoo.

There were the cheetahs he'd travelled with, watching them hunting as they'd sped off after a hapless antelope. The hyenas – chuckling, cackling, mocking him mercilessly. And then, most unpredictable of all, the short-sighted rhinos who terrified the other animals with their bad-tempered charges at anything that moved. The fastest, the meanest, the most dangerous – none of the animals had been able to tell him why he could speak Mammalogue.

Yet Adam knew that he hadn't wasted a single moment in his trips with the animals. And as he lay there in bed, his fears for the following day gradually disappeared as he imagined himself back on the African plains. The sun was slipping down towards the horizon, turning the trees to black silhouettes. A line of shifty-looking vultures were hopping along a branch. At the top of the hill opposite, a troupe of baboons were making their way to the steepest rocks, where they would be safe from any prowling predators. Away to the right, the acacia trees seemed to be floating in the mist above a distant lake, while out on the plains, the huge herds of wildebeest, zebra and gazelle continued to graze as the day slowly cooled and the light faded.

And surrounded by the awesome beauty of the scenery he had re-created in his imagination, Adam drifted off to sleep.

While they were all in the playground before going to class for the first time, Adam listened in on the friendships and rivalries as they were being revived after the long summer holiday. Apart from Ian, he didn't see anyone he knew, but he wasn't too worried about that. At least no one bothered him.

Things started to go a little wrong once he'd got to his class and the form-master, Mr Lingwood, called the register.

"Anthony Taylor."

"Here."

"Alan Tickner."

"Here."

"Stephen Tillin."

"Here."

As he heard his own name, Adam felt his cheeks and chest redden with embarrassment. All he had to say was one word, but as he opened his mouth, it disappeared.

"Adam Williams," the teacher repeated and looked up.

Everyone was staring at the boy.

"Aah, you *are* here," he said. "You're new today, aren't you?"

Adam nodded.

"Will you be having school dinners?"

He tried so hard to answer, but nothing would come, and all the while he could feel the thirty-two pairs of eyes boring into him. It was all hot and prickly inside his head as he gave it a final effort.

"Ssssandwiches."

The class erupted into laughter and began nudging one another. They had all heard that there would be some new kids from the loonie school — one of them was evidently there in the class with them.

"No school dinners," the teacher stated pedantically. "Be quiet, you lot! Peter Woods."

"Here."

Once the class had quietened down again, the rest of the morning was spent with matters of bureaucracy. The timetables for the various subjects and streams were read out and copied down. Regulations concerning minimum amounts of homework to be done were stressed. Registering times for extra-curricular subjects were given. Instructions about desks, uniform, assemblies and a multitude of other dos and don'ts were systematically gone through. Coming from the liberal 'child-is-always-right' regime of St Jude's, all of this sounded pretty daunting to Adam. A quick look around the room suggested that the majority of the class was taking the spiel somewhat less seriously than Mr Lingwood might have hoped.

The bell at ten forty-five announced the start of morning break and the class all made a dash for the playground. Adam followed behind, reluctant to leave the relative security of the classroom.

The moment he stepped into the caged and tarmacked area of the playground, he was surrounded by a mass of children eager to inspect the new kid for themselves. Boys, girls, big, small, black, white: the only thing they all had in common was a familiar taunting expression. One of the biggest pushed his way to the front and stood directly in front of Adam, feet apart, fists clenched.

"I don't think I like your face. Wants rearranging a bit, dunnit?" he said, and smirked round to his mates for approval.

Adam remained silent. He looked down at the floor.

"Oy. I'm talking to you," he shouted, poking Adam in the chest.

"I know," said Adam, looking up.

"What kind of a comment's that?" he said, shrugging theatrically. A gesture that got him a laugh. "I said I don't like your face. Whatcha gonna do about it, eh?"

"What *can* I do about it?" Adam asked. The question seemed ridiculous. He genuinely had no idea what the big, angry kid in front of him wanted him to say.

"Well, for a start," he said, triumphantly picking up on the leading question, "you could naff off back to that loonie bin where you belong. Go on, 'oppit!" he shouted, repeatedly pushing Adam off-balance.

"Don't do that," he said quietly.

"Why? What're *you* gonna do about it?"

The same question. This time, however, someone answered it for him.

"Never mind what *he*'s gonna do, you lay another finger on him and you're going the right way for a split lip."

"You 'n' whose army?"

"Don't come it, Lol, you're still in nappies."

Adam looked from Terry to the kid called Lol and back again, trying to follow what they were saying. The conversation could have been taking place in a foreign language for all he could understand. What he *had* got out of the situation was that Lol had taken a dislike to him and was trying to start a fight, and Terry had come to his defence.

"I'll do what I like," Lol sneered defiantly, and pushed Adam so hard that he lost his balance completely and landed hard on his backside.

"—in' warned you," Terry muttered through gritted teeth, landing a winding left to Lol's stomach followed by a vicious crack at his jaw.

He landed on the Tarmac a lot heavier than Adam had.

"Go on, Tel," the cry went up, as the onlookers hurriedly switched allegiances.

"What's going on?" came a deep voice from outside the circle. A moment later Mr Bateman had barged his way towards the centre. He saw Adam on the ground, Terry rubbing his knuckles and instantly leapt to the wrong conclusion.

Grabbing at Terry's collar, he half-lifted him off the ground.

"Didn't have you down for a bully, Mitchell," he said. "He's only half your size."

"It wasn't me," Terry spluttered angrily.

A ripple of "no, it wasn't him," went round the circle.

"Did Mitchell here hit you?" Mr Bateman asked Adam.

He shook his head and pointed to Lol, who was still lying on the ground in the middle of a forest of legs.

"Who's . . .? Oh, Lawrence Wilson. I might have known. Get up."

He let go of Terry's collar and helped Adam to his feet.

"You all right?"

"Yes, sir."

"You're new, aren't you?"

"Yes, sir."

"Seems I owe you an apology, Mitchell. Do you know the lad here? What's your name?"

"Adam Williams."

"Yes, sir," said Terry. "We're mates."

"Good. Right," he said, switching his attention to Lol., "Wilson, follow me. Oh, and Mitchell," he said, turning back.

"Sir?"

"Try and smarten yourself up a bit before the bell goes."

"Sir."

Adam looked at him and laughed. His own school uniform was brand-new, and looked it. It was the first one he'd ever had to wear and it felt stiff and awkward. In contrast, Terry was a complete mess: his shirt was untucked and the knot of his tie was nowhere near the collar. His parents had insisted on a start-of-term haircut, but although it was now very short it still refused to look neat, going in all directions like a storm-damaged field of wheat. And the trainers and red socks he had on were definitely not a part of the school uniform either, but presumably Mr Bateman had decided to turn a blind eye in the circumstances.

"What you grinning at then?" he asked.

"Just wondering how long it'll take for my stuff to end up like yours."

"Never," said Terry. "I'm a natural born slob."

The bell rang announcing the end of break.

"It's like a prison," said Adam. "The cage, the bells . . ."

"What? You didn't have bells at . . . where you were before?"

"No, too rigid. Interfering with our 'natural rate of educational progress'. That kind of thing."

"They still got places going there, have they?" asked Terry.

"Only for half-wits."

"Oy, none of that. You're no idiot."

"I know," said Adam, grinning. "That's why I'm here."

"You'll be all right," said Terry, heading off to his next class, hands in pockets, shoulders dipping from one side to the other with every step. "See you at lunch-time," he called back without looking round.

"See you," said Adam.

As it turned out, Terry was right. Everything was OK. Initially, it was probably a fear of the consequences they'd have to face from Terry (his 'minder', as he was dubbed) that made any potential bullies think twice about picking on Adam. But before too long, everyone forgot which school he'd come from, and he was likeable enough to make friends of his own.

Like any other kid, he was good at some subjects and not so good at others, but because of the reports that the teachers from St Jude's had sent over, the classes he was placed in were fairly accurate. The school had attempted to disguise the fact that there were top and bottom streams, so instead of lettering them from A to G, they were cryptically listed as V, I, B, G, Y, O, R. It hadn't taken long for the kids to work out that these stood for the colours of the rainbow and that Violet was the top class. Not surprisingly, the one subject where Adam was placed in the V stream was biology.

He loved it. Rabbits and gerbils were kept in the laboratory – not, he was relieved to discover, for experiments – and as he had such an obvious 'way with animals', as Mr Ashley put it, Adam was put in charge of feeding and cleaning their cages out. Sometimes, even if they didn't need anything doing to them, he would stay late after school just chatting.

'What do you think of old Ashley?' Adam asked the rabbits.

'He's all right, as owners go,' one of them replied.

'Except he will pick us up by the ears,' another one added, 'and it really hurts.'

'I can imagine,' said Adam, whose own protruding ears led to all kinds of jokers grabbing at them; usually with painful results.

'If we must be lifted, the best way is to take us gently by the scruff of the neck, and then put the other hand under our back haunches to take the weight. We'd be awfully grateful if you could let him know.'

'Don't worry, I will.'

And one day after school, he did.

"How do you know?" the teacher snapped, irritated by the boy's implied criticism.

Adam, of course, didn't want to say that they'd told him themselves, and so he came out with his standard reply.

"I read it somewhere."

"You seem to do a remarkable amount of reading," Mr Ashley said.

"About animals, I do," Adam said, innocently missing the bite in the teacher's comment.

"I've noticed."

The number of occasions that Adam's voice was heard to pipe up in disagreement when he gave some anatomical, behavioural or biological piece of information had become irritatingly frequent. So much so that he would occasionally make sure the boy was happy with what he had said before going on to the next point.

"And the longest gestation period of all is the African elephant with 640 days. If that's all right with you, Mr Williams," he would add sarcastically.

And the whole class would laugh as Adam would give the fact his serious nodded approval.

Mr Ashley had tried to turn the whole thing into a little joke, but underneath his casual exterior, he was not happy to have his authority challenged so often. The annoying part of it all was that the boy was always right. Even in the areas considered 'grey' by all the accepted works, Adam would make his assertions with such conviction that nobody doubted that he knew for sure. What particularly galled Mr Ashley was that if ever there was a dispute, the rest of the class would always note down Adam's information rather than his own.

While looking at the fauna of Australia, they had got round to the koala.

"A particularly unaggressive animal," he mentioned.

"Unless you deprive it of its eucalyptus leaves," Adam had added.

"Well, that's all it eats, isn't it?" Mr Ashley retorted. "If I took away *your* dinner, you wouldn't be too happy, would you?"

"That's not what I meant," Adam explained. The rest of the class all turned to him attentively. "The bitter shoots from the eucalyptus tree contain a chemical which makes the animal docile."

"Like a hippy on drugs, I suppose," he said, attempting to put the boy down.

"I wouldn't know about that," Adam had replied.

Infuriatingly enough, when he went to the library to check it out, the teacher found a magazine article concerning the latest discoveries of the koala's total dependence on the chemicals in the trees.

How could a thirteen-year-old be so knowledgeable? he wondered.

A similar incident had to do with elephants. Mr Ashley had trotted out the standard line that, although social animals, they remained silent for much of the time. Once again, Adam interrupted with the information that, on the contrary, they were constantly communicating, but that the sounds were too low for humans to hear. A week later, the class had all come in triumphant, having seen a programme on television which corroborated Adam's claim: the film-makers had speeded up the sound track to prove that the deep noises were really going on.

It was hardly surprising that Mr Ashley was at such a disadvantage. His knowledge stopped with books. For Adam, the facts he read were merely the starting-point. He'd discovered a long time before that a lot of theories that made their way into print were quite simply wrong. All *his* information came straight from the horse's mouth – or, if needs be, the bear's, badger's or bat's mouth. The trouble was knowing what to do with everything he had dis-covered.

'So the trips around the world with all your new animal friends are pointless, are they?' Oscar had asked the boy.

'No, they're not,' Adam conceded.

'But you don't want to discuss them.'

'Not particularly.'

Conscious that he was snapping at the cat again, Adam

rolled off the bed and sat on the floor next to her. He tickled her under her chin and couldn't help noticing how Oscar was showing her age. The eyes and fur had become dull, and her quick reactions had slowed down.

She's pushing seventy, Adam realized with a shock. A little old lady. I ought to be more considerate.

'No, not pointless,' he explained. 'I've discovered that there's no such thing as *the* most important animal. They're all totally dependent on each other – and, in turn, the mammals rely on the reptiles, the birds, the insects, the trees, the plants. All of them have both good points and bad points: the elephants are strong but vain, the cheetahs fast but impatient, the hyenas sociable but flippant. No animal is perfect, but all of them recognize that. They understand themselves and realize that for life to continue, they are all essential.

'There is only one animal that refuses to recognize this basic truth,' he continued.

'Which one?' Oscar asked. 'Let me guess. The giraffe? No, no, I know, the lion. Arrogant so-and-so's, claiming to be Lord of the Beasts and . . .'

'Not the lions,' Adam interrupted. He thought back on everything he had been told: by the fox and the hedgehog, by the bear and all the animals on the African plains, by Oscar herself. There was only one mammal which thought itself superior to the rest of the natural world. There was only one mammal which considered itself so strong and invulnerable that it treated the environment with contempt rather than respect. There was only one mammal which would take other members of the animal kingdom and experiment on them. And he, Adam, belonged to that vast species. It was a fact that didn't make him feel particularly proud.

'No, not the lions,' he repeated. 'Human beings.'

—13—
SNOW, ICE AND SMOKE

The term continued; summer turned to autumn and the leaves fell to the ground, leaving the trees bare for another winter. In the garden, Adam watched the squirrels burying their nuts and berries once more; he left out saucerfuls of food (not forgetting the pilchards) for the hedgehogs to fatten them up for the imminent hibernation; the foxes' coats grew thick in preparation for the colder months. Overhead, the twittering flocks of swallows assembled on the branches, aerials and telephone wires until one evening, when the weather and the wind direction were perfect, they all disappeared. They wouldn't be back till the following spring.

As a young boy, Adam had seen the cycle of the seasons as a series of repetitions, with each new year merely following the pattern of the one it was replacing. Now he was older, things looked very different. He knew too much about what humans were doing to their world to believe that each successive year could remain exactly the same for ever. Things were changing.

The world was being warmed up, causing the seas to rise, the polar caps to melt – the hibernating animals hardly knew what to do. The ozone layer was disappearing, the water was turning sour, the fertile soil was all blowing away. Adam knew that the sequence of seasons could no longer be relied on. As another year came to an end, instead of feeling the cycle had turned full circle, he recognized that the earth had moved one step closer to an unknown and possibly disastrous future.

"How come you're always so serious?" Tom had asked him. "Kid like you ought to be out playing football and sneaking into '18'-films. Vandalizing telephones," he added and laughed.

"I dunno," Adam shrugged.

He wanted to confide in the zoo-keeper. He felt he could trust him and there was certainly no one else he could talk to. Terry? Naima or Denise? Mr Asley? No. Occasionally he had almost brought it up, but had thought better of it. He hadn't even spoken to his mother about being able to think-speak with the animals since he was nine or so. He remembered trying to describe the way it was different from talking, but she had never really understood. And as Adam had grown older and more able to cope in the everyday world, Mammalogue had become a taboo subject between them. It was connected with all the problems he'd had as a baby and young boy. Now the problems were going, she had reasoned that the language must also have gone away – if it was ever there at all – and she wasn't about to ask whether this was actually the case.

"It's just that ... I don't know. We treat animals so badly; chaining them up, caging them in, cutting them open, taking away the places they live in. It's so unfair. And they're not stupid: they know what's happening. They've got feelings and memories just like us and . . ." Adam fell silent. He knew that his sudden impassioned outburst had gone too far, and turning round to the zoo-keeper, he grinned sheepishly.

"Sorry," he said

"Don't you apologize," Tom said. "You're right. I know you think that because I work in a zoo, I must agree with keeping animals locked up for ever. But I'd like nothing better than to let them all go back to the places where they originally came from."

"It's not that easy though," said Adam.

"Indeed it's not. As you said, their homelands are all being decimated. Where would I send them back to? Anyway, enough of that for the time being. What would you like to see now?"

"The polar bear cub," Adam answered without any hesitation.

It had been several months now since that first meeting with the keeper. They had soon become friends and Tom would take him round the zoo in his van when he wasn't too busy. Bit by bit, Adam had seen all those parts of the zoo which were kept hidden from the majority of the zoo-visitors. There were the peaceful nurseries where the pregnant females went to give birth to their young; the sick-bays where old and ailing animals were treated; the retreats where the more timid species could eat and sleep away from the prying eyes and fingers of the countless visiting tourists.

Over the months, Adam had bottle-fed an orphaned Indian elephant. He'd watched a snake wriggle clear of its discarded skin. One evening, he'd stayed after the zoo had shut to watch a female zebra delivering its gangly foal. He'd held a lion cub and a boa constrictor, a snowy owl and a wallaby, a tiny crocodile and a pink-faced chimpanzee. And once, while watching a convalescing young orang-utan, he'd suddenly had to jump back as the cheeky adolescent had leapt up on its bars and tried to pee all over his shirt.

"Nearly got you," Tom had said, and burst out laughing at the horrified expression on the boy's face.

In addition, Adam had continued his memory-trips with the animals. They'd accompanied him back to Africa, to the Australian bush, to the rain forests of South America, the Galapagos Islands, the Tibetan plateau – all over the world. Some weeks before, Adam had journeyed to the frozen wastes of northern Greenland with the polar bear. When he'd heard that she'd given birth to a tiny club, he'd had to come and see it for himself.

"The polar bear?" Tom asked, feigning surprise. "You sure?"

Adam just smiled. He always knew when Tom was teasing.

"Come on then."

Looking down into the enclosure with its landscaped system of stepped and bridged rocks, cliffs, islands and huge pool, Adam realized again that the animal's captors had tried their best to re-create an appropriate environment. Twice a day, they even dropped in massive slabs of ice, large enough for the bear to float on. At the moment, though, Mari was not out on the ice. All Adam could see was her nose and paw protruding from her cave.

'Hello,' Adam called down.

The bear shuffled forwards a little on her stomach and looked up.

'Adam,' she said, 'I've been waiting for you to turn up.'

'I can only make it at weekends during term-time,' Adam said.

'So, we're not worth skiving off for, eh?' she replied. 'In that case, I'm not sure I'm going to show you my tiny little son here.'

'Oh, please.'

'You really want to see him?'

'Stupid question. What's his name?'

'Timus.'

"Timus," Adam repeated.

"Tea what?" Tom said.

"It's his name," Adam explained. "Timus."

Tom looked at the boy. He was intrigued by the relationship Adam seemed to have with the animals. At first he'd thought it was all in the boy's head, but now he wasn't so sure. Rather than push too hard for answers, however, he had let things ride. Adam would tell him when he was good and ready.

"It's a nice name," was all he said.

And as the pair of them were still looking down into the enclosure, Mari pulled herself up on to her feet and nuzzled the tiny cub towards the front of the cave. Timus was tiny. Snowier than his yellow-white mother, he looked like a dumpy little puppy. Finding himself outside, he screwed his nose up slightly and looked round, squeaking with fear and excitement.

'There's Adam,' Mari thought, looking up at the boy. 'He can speak Mammalogue and one day . . . who knows?'

'Mallamogue,' the weeny cub tried to repeat. 'Mammaladamogue. Mallamadamogue. Hi!'

'Hiya, Timus,' Adam thought back happily.

"Where's Thal?" he asked Tom.

"In the next enclosure. Even in the wild, the males will sometimes eat their cubs, so they have to be separated."

'Is that true?' Adam asked Mari.

''fraid so,' she agreed. 'Don't you remember the denning

157

area where I was brought up? My father was miles away down on the sea-ice hunting seals.'

'Yes,' Adam nodded. 'I do remember.'

His particular interest in the ice bears had started with one of Mr Ashley's lessons. The biology teacher had been pointing out that although they were a member of the family of *ursidae*, they differed in various ways. For a start, unlike all other bears, their paws were hairy on the bottom to help them walk over the slippery ice. Also, in contrast to the rest of the species, animal flesh constituted a major part of their diet. Adam was quite happy with these pieces of information. On the matter of hibernation, however, he was far from sure that Mr Ashley had his facts right. Even the film he showed of the bears apparently emerging after the long, dark Arctic night failed to convince Adam.

The only way to find out once and for all was to go and ask the animal itself. And that was precisely what he did.

The trip had confirmed what he had suspected and the following week, Adam had sat in the class wondering whether to tell Mr Ashley about his latest findings. In the end, he decided that he didn't have enough concrete evidence to persuade him — anyway, *he* knew and that was enough. It did make him wonder how much of the information the teachers gave out was accurate though. If he'd been able to travel back in time to famous battles and revolutions, how many of Mr Richards' so-called facts would he have been able to expose? And if it were possible to become fantastically large or infinitesimally small, how many of Mrs Padgett's ideas of physics would have crumbled away to nothing? Teachers could spoonfeed the kids just about anything and they would swallow it whole.

'Timus will probably never see the real Arctic, will he?' Adam asked Mari.

'I doubt it,' she replied. 'Still, at least no one will shoot him here. Anyway, they've turned the place I was brought up into a huge mining-town. That was why I was brought here – they found me snooping round the dustbins looking for my old den.'

Adam sighed.

"What is it?" Tom asked.

"I was just thinking of Timus," he said. "A polar bear who'll never see the poles."

"Well, at least no one will shoot him," Tom said.

"I know, that's what Ma . . ." Adam stopped himself just in time. He still wasn't ready to let the keeper in on his secret just yet.

"You hungry?" he said, ignoring Adam's interrupted sentence.

"Yeah."

"Come on then."

Adam liked eating at the Hutchinsons' place. It was noisy and friendly, unlike his own house where his father's oppressive presence so often spoilt the atmosphere. Tom lived in a bungalow just inside the zoo-gates with his wife Ally, and the two kids, Em and Roland. Although they were only five and two, Adam loved being with them. They were as lively and playful as a couple of young cubs. When he'd first met Roly, he'd tried communicating with him in Mammalogue, and to his surprise the baby had answered. It hadn't been totally fluent, but the language was unmistakably there. The pair of them had sat swapping tales about the zoo animals and giggling over the nonsense that adults would say to babies whenever they saw them. By the time his first human words came, however, Roland had already totally lost the ability to speak his mammal language. It had just been a brief phase, a reminder of human beings' animal past, like gills and a tail that babies would have for a few days while they were forming in the womb.

It had occurred to Adam that perhaps he wasn't so strange after all — the only difference was that he had held on to Mammalogue when all those around him had forgotten it.

"Come and see us again soon," Ally would always say, as he left after lunch.

"I will," Adam answered.

And riding back to his own home, he compared the way the two little children would rush out to greet their father with the state of indifference which had developed between him and Derek. Looking back on it, he realized that it must have been hard for his father, having such an unresponsive son. But it wasn't Adam's fault that he had heard only the animals' voices, and his father had certainly made no effort to understand *him*. It was like the bright Arctic sky reflecting the snow back against itself, becoming more and more intensely blue. Derek's naturally withdrawn nature had been exaggerated by Adam's inability to communicate, and now that the boy could respond to other human beings, it was too late.

Winter was mild that year. Compared with his visit to the icy land of the polar bears, anything would have seemed mild to Adam, of course, but even for Britain, the weather was warm. It didn't snow once and the daffodils and crocuses were up before the end of January. Dazed and confused, the hedgehogs and dormice emerged from their burrows and nests even though the days were still so short. By Easter, it was hot enough to go out in just a T-shirt, and Adam, Terry, Dexter and the rest had started meeting up over the park after school again.

"Roberts is hopeless," Terry was saying.

"Is he heck! S'pose you'd like Baker in," said Dexter.

"Well, at least he can control the ball, not like the useless jerk you've got."

"Useless! He scored twenty-eight goals this season."

"What about Kenley?" Ian suggested.

At last, Terry and Dexter had something they could agree on.

"Kenley's rubbish!" they both shouted.

They were discussing the team that the England manager *should* have got together for the qualifying match against Italy – the team *they* would have picked if anyone'd had the common sense to ask them.

Adam was sitting there with them on the park bench, half-listening, half-wondering whether the 'old' Oscar would ever return. The car accident certainly seemed to have undermined her confidence. At least, Adam assumed the accident was to blame, though perhaps there was another cause for her change of temperament. Something she was keeping from him. Whatever it might be, she had certainly become peevish and detached, and when she moved, the spring in her step had all but disappeared.

Then again, he reminded himself, she was getting on. Adam worked out that she was nearly seventy-three, which was a lot older than his grandma.

"Well, what about Lloyd then?"

"Not much good in the air, is he?"

They were still no nearer their dream team when Naima and Denise came running up.

"Afternoon, girls," said Terry.

"Naima's cat's gone," Denise blurted out immediately.

"What, Smoke?" said Ian.

Naima nodded.

"There was a thing in the paper the other week warning people to keep their pets in," said Dexter. "There's some gang going round nicking them."

"Well, what are they doing with them?" Terry asked.

"Fur coats, my dad reckons," Dexter answered.

Naima burst into tears.

"Oh, well done, Dex," Denise said. "*Really* subtle."

"Sorry, Naim," he said quietly. "They won't have taken Smoke. She'll be back this evening, I bet you."

"But what if she isn't?" Naima asked. "There's masses of them gone missing. And none of them turn up."

"If I could get my hands on those . . ." Terry muttered.

"We ought to set up a Pet Patrol," said Ian. "Take it in turns to keep an eye out for anything out of the ordinary, like."

"They're out all night," said Dexter. "Driving round, one o'clock, two o'clock, when no one's about."

"You seem to know a lot about it," said Terry.

"'swhat I heard."

"Well, we gotta try something," Ian persisted. "What do you reckon, Adam?"

They all turned to him. He might not know that much about football, but whenever any questions about animals cropped up, they always knew where to go. Adam, for his part, hadn't so far said a word. Perhaps there was some money to be had in turning pet cats into fur coats. If it was dyed, they could probably pass it off as cony or fox. In one way, he hoped that was what was happening. The alternative was too horrible to contemplate.

"I don't know," he said. "Smoke was a lovely cat. You can get a lot of money for a Burmese. Perhaps someone stole her to sell her to someone else."

"I wouldn't mind that so much," Naima sniffed. "As long as . . . as long . . ." she started crying again.

"Here, cheer up, Naim," Denise said, putting her arm round her shoulder. "Come back to my place. I'll get you a milk-shake."

The two of them wandered off, leaving the boys sitting on the bench making plans. The selection of the England team, which they were powerless to alter, suddenly became irrelevant in the face of the spate of local petnapping which perhaps, just perhaps, they *could* do something about. Complicated schemes were dreamt up, one after the other, received a brief burst of enthusiasm before being dismissed as either impractical, dangerous or just plain stupid. Dexter suggested attaching radio transmitters to their collars, but if they were taken off in a van, they'd never be able to keep track of the signal. Ian suggested a complicated system of trip-wires and cameras. But as none of them knew where they could lay their hands on the equipment, that idea fizzled out. Terry suggested stuffing a dead cat full of explosives so that when the gang tried to drive off with the booby-trapped moggy in the back of their van, it would blow up.

"Yeah, well we'll have to think about that one," Dexter sniggered.

"Don't call us . . ." Ian added.

As it started to get dark, they wandered back to the edge of the park and went their separate ways, all promising to come up with a really good idea by the following day. Adam went straight up to his bedroom, where Oscar was lying on his bed.

'Os, have you heard anything about cats disappearing?' he asked.

'I haven't been out for ages,' Oscar replied. 'Why?'

''Cos loads of them have been going recently, and now Naima's cat Smoke is missing as well.'

Oscar remained silent.

'What'll you do if I find out?' she asked finally.

'How do you mean?'

'Well, will you try and stop the people doing it, or call the police? Or get your friend Tom to help you? Or what? I don't want you getting hurt.'

'I thought I'd get the RSPCA on to it.'

The cat nodded thoughtfully.

'All right,' she thought, 'as long as the weather's not too bad tomorrow, I'll go and make a few inquiries.'

'Thanks, Oscar,' Adam thought back.

He looked back at the cat as he left the room. She was obviously very troubled about something, but was making a special effort not to let her thoughts slip out in Mammalogue. Adam remembered what he'd been thinking in the park, and wondered whether Oscar had had the same hideous premonition about where the missing pets might have ended up. If that was the case, all he could do was hope that both of them were wrong.

—14—
OSCAR'S FINAL WORDS

It often happens that, quite spontaneously, a whole group of people is thinking of the same thing without realizing it. A chance gesture, or word, or remark will suddenly trigger off a chain reaction of responses which leads to everyone discovering what they had half-suspected all along. This happened to Class 4 during their biology lesson on 18 May. Mr Ashley had been dealing with rodents, from the tiny shrew to the massive capybara, but it was a comment he happened to make towards the end of the lesson that got everyone talking that lunch-time.

"The interesting thing about rodents is their remarkable fertility," he was saying. "The number of predators they have requires this, of course. But let us assume that there are no predators, that there is no shortage of food, that the climatic conditions are ideal – has anyone a clue as to how many descendants one healthy pair of rats would have after three years?"

Various figures flew around the room, but Mr Ashley continued to shake his head smugly.

"No, no. The answer, believe it or not, is twenty million. Twenty million! Can you imagine it?"

Everyone agreed that they could not.

"Which is why," he continued as the bell went, "they are the ideal animal for scientific experiments. No one has to go out and find them, they just breed them to order."

As one, the class remembered two pieces of information which they had previously been keeping totally separate. The first was the awareness that Dimwell's Research Institute was on the outskirts of the town. The second was that, for the last couple of months, pets had been disappearing at an alarming rate. Mr Ashley's innocent words had brought the two thoughts together and instantly a new concept was born.

Dimwell's was carrying out experiments on the local pets.

Everyone in the school knew someone whose cat or dog or rabbit had mysteriously gone missing and, before the end of the lunch-break, it was being treated as common knowledge that the research institute was responsible. The usual conversations about the top-ten records, the previous night's episodes of the 'soaps', and the more local who-was-going-out-with-who gossip were all suspended as the initial rumours about Dimwell's became hard facts.

"They squirt shampoo into their eyes. I mean, how would you like that?"

"'s horrible. And they test all these new drugs on them."

"*And* diseases. Like cancer and Aids."

"Yeah, they inject all this bacteria into them and then try and cure them. And if the drug doesn't work then they die, and if it *does* work then they keep using it anyway to find out how much you need for an overdose."

"So they can't win."

"No, once they're in there, that's it."

"And I heard they cut them open."

"They do. They experiment on their brains."

"When they're still alive."

"Well, it's not right, is it?"

"What would you do if they got hold of Sookie."

"Or Vic?"

"If they took Vic I'd go nutty. Kill someone."

"That wouldn't do any good."

"Well, what *can* we do then?"

Around the playground, in their small groups, the kids argued through just what needed to be done, firstly to prove that the pets *were* there, and secondly to get them out again. Letters to the local paper, phone calls to the police, a petition to their MP, a demonstration in front of Dimwell's front gates which would then get into the national press, a kamikaze bombing-mission on the entire complex: the suggestions became increasingly extreme. Though, in the end, the kamikaze idea was only thrown out as it would injure and kill the very animals they were planning on saving.

"Well, what about the people who work there?"

"Superglue the locks shut."

"What, to the institute or their cars?"

"BOTH!"

"Letter bombs."

"No, that sort of thing is horrible. You see it on the news. It's stupid. You can't fight violence with violence."

"'s no worse than what they're doing to the animals."

"Anyway, you always hurt the wrong people."

"Who *are* the people there, anyway?"

"Who knows someone that works there? Eh?"

Adam hadn't said a single word throughout the increasingly heated discussions. Squirming with embarrassment, he was trying his best not even to *think* about his father's job at Dimwell's, just in case someone read his mind. These days, he was as ashamed of his father as Derek had once been of his apparently handicapped baby son. More so, for Adam had never had any option about the way he was born; his father chose to work where he did.

The bell went and Adam breathed a deep sigh of relief. He had been spared.

But not for long. The suspicions about the institute refused to go away and the children's concerns led to impromptu discussions being held in the classrooms about drug testing, vivisection and animal rights. A couple of the parents did write to the local press, and a petition was organized in the centre of town to express 'the concern' of the undersigned and to demand an inquiry into the goings-on at Dimwell's. Two thousand, eight hundred and fifteen signatures were collected that first Saturday.

Adam remained nervous about the whole situation. Having overcome the difficulties of changing from his Special School to the local comprehensive, the last thing he needed was to be picked on because of his father's job. Whenever he met up with Terry and the gang after school, the conversation would always get round to Dimwell's and what they were going to do about the place. And every time he would have to pretend he knew nothing at all about the institute. It was all becoming too much for him. He had to talk to someone and there was only one person who he came close to trusting enough.

"Tom," Adam said.

"Good grief," he replied, "so the boy has got a tongue after all."

It was Saturday, and Adam had decided to cycle over to the zoo. He'd found the keeper cleaning out the reindeer paddock on the far side of the zoo and proceeded to help him with his work, dragging in the huge branches of beech leaves for the deer to nibble on and filling the troughs with fresh water. Adam liked the reindeer, with their huge, comical feet and top-heavy antlers.

On a previous visit they had told him a legend about why their bodies were so strangely proportioned.

Adam had made a note of the story, and subsequently written it up for his monthly 'Animal Tale' in the local newspaper. In turn, he had amused the animals with the human tales of flying reindeer pulling Santa's sleigh at Christmas, and about Rudolph, the special leader of the herd, with the bright red, headlamp nose.

"I'm still waiting," Tom said, as they climbed back into his van. "What did you want to ask me?"

And Adam poured his heart out about the research institute and the disappearing pets and the kids at school and the fact that he felt really guilty because his father worked there. It was such a relief just talking about it. And when Tom reassured him that he was in no way responsible for his father and that the boy should do what his conscience was telling him was right, Adam felt as if a great heavy burden had been lifted from his shoulders. He still hadn't decided exactly what to do, but at least he now knew that he could.

"Thanks," he said and wished more strongly than ever that, rather than his own father, he had Tom for a dad. And yet with those feelings came the inevitable guilt. Derek wasn't *that* bad and likely as not all the fears and rumours about Dimwell's would turn out to be totally unfounded.

"Now," said Tom, "I've got a surprise for you. When we stop, I want you to close your eyes."

He did as he was told and let himself be led to one of the animal houses. At first, he wasn't quite sure where he was: either apes or reptiles. As they went through the revolving

169

door, the sound of chattering and squealing left him in no doubt.

"Saty!" he yelled and couldn't keep his eyes shut a moment longer.

"She had a boy," Tom called out as Adam ran off to the far end of the hall where the chimpanzees were kept.

There, snuggled up in Saty's arms, was the tiniest baby chimp Adam had ever seen. He stared at the pale fingers: so small that the skin seemed to hang off the bones like rubber gloves. And the little ears. And the feet clutching hold of the mother's fur.

'He's called Pan,' Saty thought to Adam, looking up. 'Beautiful, isn't he?'

Adam simply nodded.

'My seventh,' she added. 'The seventh wee one I've given birth to.'

'You don't sound that happy.'

'No? A mixture of sadness and happiness perhaps. You never know what sort of life you're inflicting on a baby when you bring it into the world, do you?'

Tom looked at Adam. He had still not challenged him about his relationship with the animals. Clearly it was very close though, and seeing the boy and the chimpanzee apparently deep in silent conversation, he decided to leave them well alone.

"I'll be back later," he said.

Adam didn't hear. He was already being taken back to the community at the base of the mountain where Saty had been born. Although he loved seeing all the places the animals showed him, Adam remained especially fond of Africa. He loved the wide, warm expanse of the savannah grasslands and even here to the west, in the thick, tropical lakeside forests, he felt that bizarre sensation once again of 'coming home'.

'There were about fifty of us,' the younger, more agile chimp of Saty's memory was recounting. 'And it was quite idyllic.'

'I can see that,' Adam replied. 'It's wonderful.'

Over by the bushes, three of the young chimps were playing a game that looked like a form of complicated tag. In front of them, a group of older apes were sitting on the ground sociably, touching each other gently, clasping hands, kissing lips and grooming one another's coats with nimble fingers. A youngster sitting with its mother grew nervous when a grown male joined the group. It stretched out its hand tentatively, and the male kissed it on the back reassuringly.

The broad-leaved trees provided a thick cover over the clearings where the group of chimpanzees played in the dappled shadows. Clearly highly intelligent, Adam watched as one took a thin piece of straw, trimmed it down to size and used it to draw out termites from their holes. Another used a long stick as a weapon against a baboon three times its size. A third fashioned a tool out of a pointed twig, and with it speared a banana which remained obstinately just out of reach.

'But why have you brought me here?' Adam asked.

'Be patient.'

Saty led the boy away from the main community and down a rocky track running alongside a stream. It emerged in a dusty clearing. Adam sensed something wrong, but couldn't put his finger on what exactly it was. He noticed Saty staring at him intently.

'What has happened here?' he asked nervously.

'This is where it took place.'

'What?'

'We should have known it was all a trick — that bananas didn't just grow in boxes. But . . .' she began to sob tearlessly.

'But what happened?' Adam asked.

'You'll see,' she said. 'I've brought you back to the time, ten minutes before they arrived. If we go up this tree here, where I was resting, you'll get a clear view of everything.'

From his concealed vantage-point high up in the tree, Adam watched as a group of four men tramped their way noisily into the undergrowth and secured twelve heavy boxes to the ground. Having filled them with bananas, they primed the trap doors and retreated to wait. Word soon went round the group of chimps that instead of having to forage for something to eat as they did every other day, lunch on this particular afternoon had come to them. The chimps went wild with excitement and whooped and screamed as they discovered more and more of the apparently abandoned bananas.

The largest apes were able to reach in to remove the food. For the younger ones this was not possible. They had to climb right inside, which was precisely what the trappers had been banking on, as it was those smaller adolescents that they were after. As soon as their feet touched the bottom of the box, the trap door was released and one after another, the chimpanzees were imprisoned inside.

'That was my brother, Tyrus,' she noted sadly as the fourth of the boxes slammed shut. 'I'll have to take you back to the zoo now, it's my turn soon.'

'But you don't have to go,' Adam protested. 'You know what's going to happen, so avoid it.'

'I can't,' Saty thought back. 'It's impossible to change what's already happened. And anyway, even if I could, what would happen to you if I did that?'

Adam realized what she meant. If she wasn't caught, she couldn't have been sent to the zoo, which meant she couldn't return him – but then if she wasn't there, how could he have come here? His head began to reel. All he knew was that given the choice between the idyllic family life of the chimpanzees and the tense home atmosphere he himself had grown up in, he would take the former any day. As Saty began to hurry him along, he realized it wasn't a choice he had open to him.

Below him, the eleventh of the dozen boxes slammed shut. The sound of the imprisoned chimps screaming in fury and terror echoed round the jungle.

'Quick, quick,' Saty urged him, grabbing hold of his hand. 'You'll have to leave. NOW!'

'But what's going to happen to you?'

'You know what. I was lucky, I ended up in the zoo, unlike . . .'

Before she could finish her sentence, the ear-splitting screeching began to recede, the deep, mottled green of the jungle faded away and, as Adam blinked, he found himself back in the Ape House, looking back down at the older Saty with her infant, Pan, clutched to her breast.

'I hate even thinking about it,' she admitted, looking up at him miserably.

'You *were* captured then?'

'I had to be.'

Adam looked from side to side. He knew that he wouldn't like the answer, but he couldn't push the question away.

'What did happen to the others?' he asked quietly.

Saty looked straight at him with her deep, dark, sad eyes and shuddered.

'They took them away,' she said slowly, 'to England, to Germany, to the United States and France.'

'To zoos?'

Saty shook her head.

'No, to scientific laboratories. They were all injected with different bacteria, different viruses. Smallpox, polio, syphilis – you see, we are very like you physiologically. Our blood reactions are similar, tissues can be grafted, we produce antibodies to combat disease in the same way. It makes perfect human sense to try out their new drugs on us before themselves.'

Adam remained silent. Whenever he'd seen chimpanzees before, in zoos and in the wild, he had always been struck by how similar they were to human beings. Now he was not so sure. Perhaps humans acted like chimpanzees in some respects, but the opposite could never ever be true.

'And that's why I'm so worried about little Pan here,' she thought, clutching him all the tighter. 'If I thought I'd brought him into the world so that he could be taken away and experimented on, I . . .'

'They won't,' Adam thought back defiantly. "They wouldn't, they couldn't."

"Couldn't what?" a voice behind him asked.

Adam realized he'd been thinking aloud. He turned round. Tom was back and was looking at the boy worriedly.

"The chimps here," he said. "They won't be sent to laboratories, will they? That wouldn't be fair. They couldn't take them away from their mothers to do experiments on them, could they?"

"Hey, calm down," Tom said, "calm down."

"Well, will they?" Adam demanded, fighting back the tears.

"No animals that come here or are born here are ever sent to laboratories. Ever," he added.

"Promise?"

"You have my solemn word. Good grief, Adam, you must realize that's against everything I stand for?"

"I know," Adam said, looking up. "I'm sorry, it's just . . ."

But he didn't want to relate Saty's story. And he didn't want to admit how frightened it had made him that his father might be involved in the disappearance of the local pets. It was too horrible a thought even to contemplate.

"It doesn't matter. I know you're upset. Let's go."

As they were walking away, Adam heard a whispered voice in his head.

'Thank you,' it said. 'Thank you so much.'

And he turned round to see Saty looking at him leave. He could have sworn she was smiling.

The cycle-ride home that day took longer than usual. He'd turned down the offer of a lift with Tom because he hadn't wanted to talk, but now, pedalling along, he couldn't stop thinking about Dimwell's. For all the arguments and counter-arguments that were noisily battling it out in his head, he might just as well have gone in the van.

On the one hand, as the laboratories needed a constant supply of larger animals, it made sense for them to steal them from the local area. On the other, it was stupid of them as it would be bound to raise suspicion. But, there again, it could be private individuals doing it for a bit of extra cash — and as Dimwell's was owned by the Ministry of Defence, any investigation would be difficult to arrange. But if they did find out that the pets were going there, what would happen to Derek Williams? The prospect alarmed Adam. He was his father, after all.

And as always happened, the more he thought, the slower he pedalled. It was almost three hours after he'd set off when he finally reached the outskirts of the town. As he made his way along the road at the bottom of the park, the arguments *against* Dimwell's having abducted the pets had more or less won. In the end it was Oscar who had swung the decision. As she had promised Adam earlier in the week, she had gone out to make inquiries with the other animals in the area about whether they knew anything about the disappearing pets. She had drawn a blank. If anyone knew about Dimwell's, Oscar was certain to.

"Hey!"

"Oy, Winger!"

Adam turned round to see who had called out. It was Denise and Ian belting along the pavement behind him, waving their arms frantically.

"What is it?" he asked.

"It's Vic," they shouted. "Vic's gone."

"Vic?" Adam repeated. Surely no one would chance stealing such a big dog.

"He was chained up outside the house last night, and when they woke up this morning, he was gone. Someone had smashed the lock open."

"Where's Terry?"

"He's over in the park. Been looking for him all day, he has."

Adam got off his bike and followed the others. When they found Terry, it was clear from his red, puffy eyes that he had been crying. It was also clear that his despair had since turned to anger.

"I'll kill 'em," he yelled, clenching his fist and thumping the back of the bench. "I will. They're dead men."

"But you don't know . . ." Adam started.

"Course we know. Who are you trying to cover up for?"

Adam knew that the question meant nothing, that it had only been asked in thoughtless anger, but it put him on his guard nevertheless. He'd have to be careful what he said.

"And I'll tell you what," Terry continued. "We're going along there and we're going to smash our way in and let all those animals go. D'ya hear me? All of 'em."

"You bet," Ian said.

"But how?" Adam asked.

"Are you with us or what?" Terry yelled. "'Cos if not, then naff off!"

"Course I'm with you," said Adam.

"But?"

"But, well, I've been there before. They've got a really tall fence, barbed wire, spotlights, armed guards, trained dogs . . . we're . . . Well, look at us."

"Just needs good planning," said Terry, subdued but still stubborn.

"You're right," Ian agreed, nodding enthusiastically. "I'm still for it."

"OK," said Adam wearily.

"Let's meet up here tomorrow at eleven," said Terry. "We'll get things sorted then."

Adam pushed his bike the rest of the way home. He could feel himself being dragged into something he knew he was going to regret. His father would never forgive him if he heard he was part of some gang hell-bent on breaking into the institute. Having locked the bike up at the back of the garage, he wandered miserably back down the garden path. It had been a horrible day, he thought. He'd be glad when it was over.

"Oh, Adam, I am glad you're back," Miriam said to him as he opened the kitchen door. "I was so afraid you'd be . . ."

"Oscar!" he yelled, hearing her weak and plaintive little voice calling out for him.

He rushed up the stairs and into his bedroom. Oscar was lying in her basket, wheezing gently.

"Nooo!" Adam moaned quietly. "Not now. Not today."

'Sorry,' Oscar thought.

'Oh, don't be silly,' he thought back. 'That's not what I meant.'

Miriam stood in the doorway as her son hugged the little animal that had helped him so much all through his childhood. She felt so useless. So excluded.

'It's all my fault, isn't it?' Adam was thinking. 'My fault. I made you go out in the cold and check with all those other animals. If only I hadn't. If only . . .'

'Adam . . .'

'I'm so sorry,' he continued. 'I didn't . . .'

'Adam, listen to me,' the cat insisted. 'I wasn't totally honest with you the other day. I shouldn't have lied but, well, I didn't want to upset you.'

'What about?' Adam asked, gently stroking the wheezing cat.

'About . . . about, what I found out. Adam, the pets that are all disappearing, the cats and dogs, rabbits and guinea pigs, they *are* going to Dimwell's.'

Adam felt icy shivers shooting up and down his back.

'But . . .'

'Ssh,' Oscar instructed. 'You always were one for interrupting. Just let me finish. I . . . that is, when I was knocked down that time – you know where I was found. Well, I'd been to . . .'

'Where?' Adam asked, dreading the answer he knew he was about to hear.

'Dimwell's. They were taken there, Adam,' she sighed. 'All my kittens. Every one of them. They were all taken there.'

She closed her eyes. The wheezing stopped.

PART
TWO

—15—
THE BEST-LAID PLANS

Adam sat staring out to sea. He had been there since early that morning, as he had been there the day before and the day before that. Everything was so quiet. It was miles away from the traffic, the crowds and the hustle-bustle of town life. Seagulls soared and wheeled overhead, wrasse and rocklings swam around his dangling feet. Hour after hour he would spend every day, watching the sun passing slowly across the sky, turning the still water pink and turquoise as it sank down towards the horizon.

It is so calm, so beautiful here, and yet even now, months after he and his mother came to stay in the tiny cottage with Aunt Lucy, it is all still there. Under the calm surface, hideous memories are seething furiously. They will not show themselves. They will not go away.

Adam had always known that Oscar would die long before him. That was the problem with friendships taking place between members of two species. Almost every mammal is allotted 800,000,000 heartbeats during its life-time. From the largest to the smallest of the mammals this is the case. The elephant, with twenty-five beats per minute, takes sixty years to reach its limit, while the tiny shrew, its heart racing at ten beats every second, completes its hurried life after only two and a half years. By the time Adam had reached the age of fourteen, Oscar had already used up her allowance.

Knowing this was bound to happen, however, hadn't made the loss of his 'Protector' any easier. And even if he'd been able to accept that her nine lives had all been used up at last, those final words she'd whispered to him had made her death a thousand times worse.

"No. NO. NO!!!" he had shouted, his voice getting louder and louder. As his mother had tried to comfort him he had sworn and screamed, whipping himself up into an uncontrollable tantrum. Miriam had feared that he was regressing to the state he'd been locked into as a toddler, before she had first brought Oscar to the house. She felt inadequate, frustrated by the ludicrous situation of not being able to take the place of a cat. But as she listened more carefully to the torrent of abusive language, she realized that it wasn't Oscar's death alone which had so upset him.

"The liar!" he was screaming. "The cruel, evil monster!"

It made no sense to her, and all she could do was hold the distraught boy closely and pray that he would calm down. When, in due course, the sobbing and screaming did finally subside, she assumed he was over the worst. But she was wrong. The nightmare sequence of events was only just beginning.

The sea continued to lap around Adam's toes. He swirled his feet around and watched a startled crab scuttle back to the safety of a rock. Somewhere in the distance was the gentle music he had heard all those years ago. A soft, hushing melody, constantly changing, never repeating. He wondered vaguely what could be making the sound, but before reaching any conclusions, his memory had taken him back to the scene he kept going over and over in his mind.

"So you're with us, are you?" Terry had said.

"Yes."

"Good."

Together, over the next few days, the six of them planned exactly what they were going to do. Initially, they'd thought it might be a good idea to involve as many people as possible in the break-in, so that by sheer volume of numbers they'd be able to overpower the guards. But, in the end, because they knew that someone was bound to give the game away, they limited it to the gang of six. Terry was in charge of obtaining some wire-cutters from his dad's tool-kit, Naima was to get some string and wire from her mother's shop, Dexter and Ian were assigned the task of bringing rope, cameras and flashlights, while Denise was to get the names of a couple of local journalists who could be phoned up on the night to cover whatever happened.

Adam said he'd see to the guard dogs. None of the others knew what he intended to do, but he looked so determined and confident that they didn't press him for details.

The raid on the Dimwell Institute was planned for the following Sunday night. Firstly, because no one except for the three security guards would be working there, and secondly, because it would burst on to the headlines at the beginning of the week.

At least, that was what they hoped.

*

The sea was growing choppier. The tide had turned now, and the wind direction with it. Angry grey-red clouds on the horizon were being swept towards the shore. Adam leant back and felt the chill wind slapping him in the face.

He remained deaf to the creature below the surface of the water, but it was there, watching him. Hidden from view, it gazed with deep, sympathetic eyes at the boy. It had returned day after day for months to monitor the boy's progress, waiting for the right moment to appear to him.

Not yet, but soon.

Standing behind the thick wire fence which enclosed the research institute, the six kids looked at one another and wondered whether they shouldn't simply cut their losses and give up now. With the coils of barbed wire, the brightly lit no man's land patrolled by the guards and dogs, the place looked impenetrable.

"Now what?" Terry had said.

It was the question the others were asking themselves, but hadn't wanted to say out loud.

"We go in," Ian answered with nervous bravado.

"And then?"

It was Adam who took over. The awful atmosphere of pain emanating from the buildings in the complex was beginning to overwhelm him again. He knew there was no alternative. Having committed himself to being there, he was not about to give up without a fight now. He looked through the fence at the dogs. They were trotting behind the guards, obediently at heel. Clearly, they had been rigidly trained to respond to the orders given to them by their human masters. And yet, they remained animals. Adam could only hope that Mammalogue would work.

"So what are you going to do?" Dexter whispered.

"Ssssh!" Terry said. He could see the same glazed concentration coming over Adam's face that he'd noticed when Vic had been stuck in the tunnel.

'Hey!' Adam thought to the two dogs.

They ignored him.

'Over here,' he tried again.

Still there was nothing. Perhaps they *had* lost the ability to speak Mammalogue after all.

'You German shepherds,' Adam persisted, 'I'm talking to you. Yes, *YOU!*'

The two of them looked round to see where the strange voice was coming from, alerting the guards.

"Can you hear something, lad?" one of them said.

'Don't make it obvious!' Adam thought back. 'I need to talk to you, but just keep walking as though you can't hear me.'

'What's all this about?' one of the dogs asked. It sounded suspicious but did as Adam had requested.

He realized he was going to have to be very careful. They were so mindlessly loyal. If he thought the wrong thing to the dogs, they would simply bark the alarm. Reasoning with them probably wouldn't work – they had been trained to obey without questioning. No, the only way Adam would be able to get them to co-operate was to frighten them.

'You know what happens to guard dogs when they become old, soft and slow, don't you?' he asked. 'They're experimented on,' he continued, without waiting for an answer, 'to find out what made them so obedient in the first place.'

'What do you mean?'

Interest: it was exactly the response Adam had hoped for.

'I mean, they'll use you while you're young and fierce, but the moment your teeth start falling out, you'll be on the inside of that building, not the outside.'

Adam felt the dogs shudder.

'And once you're in there, you'll never be let out, will you?' he added. 'Or do they sometimes release the animals?'

'No,' the dogs thought back.

"What're we waiting for?" Ian asked.

Adam impatiently motioned him to keep quiet. Then, he mimed a scissors action with his fingers to let Terry know it was time to start cutting a hole in the fence. The gradual persuading of the dogs continued bit by bit. In some ways, Adam felt sorry for them. He was forcing them to choose between the animals locked up inside and the humans who had trained them, fed them and looked after them kindly since they were helpless puppies. Adam understood the dilemma they were being confronted with only too well. He looked around at the car-park and was relieved to see that his father's car wasn't there.

'We can't let you in,' one of the dogs replied. 'It's more than our job's worth.'

'Fair enough, if that's where you feel your loyalties lie,' Adam answered. 'But I promise that you'll live to regret it.'

He watched the two dogs looking at each other. The guards had stopped and one of them was offering the other a cigarette.

'You *know* what they do to animals in there,' Adam persisted. 'Is that what you want for yourselves?'

The dogs growled.

"Hey, what is it with you two this evening," one of the guards asked, patting his dog on the head.

"Getting old," the other guard replied, totally unaware that this throwaway comment would seal the fate of both him and the entire institute.

'See what I mean?' Adam leapt in. 'D'ya hear that? They're just waiting for those giveaway signs that you're past your prime and then you'll be inside, on the slab and being cut open before you can say Rin Tin Tin.'

The dogs sat there, their tongues lolling over their teeth. They didn't look as though anything had changed, but even though they could certainly hear the gentle *click click* of the wire-cutters snipping a big hole in the perimeter fence, they weren't responding to it. Adam knew that he had won them over.

'All you've got to do is disarm them,' he said. 'Do to them what you've been trained to do to any intruders. We'll do the rest.'

Adam gave the command. An instant later the other kids saw the first proof that he'd been doing something other than just staring into mid-air. Both dogs suddenly leapt up and began growling, barking and baring their teeth at the two guards.

"What the . . .?" one of them spluttered, dropping his cigarette and backing off.

"Down, you stupid dog. Down!" the other one ordered.

Confronted with the fear and anger in their masters' voices, the dogs were confused. All their lives they had been trained not to bite the hand that feeds them. Adam watched them anxiously.

The third guard emerged with his dog from the side of the building to see what all the commotion was about. As the door opened, a cacophonous bedlam from within filled the air. There were cats yowling, dogs howling and monkeys screeching – all of them responding in terror and excitement to the disturbance they could sense going on outside. It was this cry of hysterical anticipation that the guard dogs reacted to.

As the third man tried to make a run for it, all three of the huge dogs made a lunge at their masters. They bit hold of their sleeves and dragged them down to the ground, where they snarled viciously into their faces. The guards, who had taught the dogs all they knew, remained motionless.

They realized that one sudden movement could be their last.

"Come on," yelled Adam, pushing down the loose section of fencing and rushing in. "Ian, Dexter, you get that one, Terry, you tie these two together."

'Good dogs. Well done,' Adam thought gratefully as he patted and petted the guard dogs. 'Well done, all of you!'

With the three guards gagged, tied up and being watched by the three German shepherds, Adam nervously led the way to the main entrance. Every step he took filled him with a mounting sense of dread as, the nearer he got, the louder the sound of the petrified animals became.

No unauthorized person was meant to get this far unchallenged. Adam turned the handle of the door and pushed. It wasn't locked.

The sky above him was now the colour of slate. The rising tide was being stirred up by the squally winds, and frothy waves were slapping against the jetty. Adam continued to look straight ahead of him. He could no longer see where the sea stopped and the sky began as they blended together in a grey-green mist.

How many times had he relived those moments leading up to the door of the institute?

He wasn't sure.

Time after time, the whole scene had been repeated. The persuading of the dogs, the cutting of the fence, the tying-up of the men and then, with the inevitability of a recurring nightmare, he would find himself walking up the steps to the unlocked door.

It was so tempting to turn around and go back again. To leave the door shut and walk away. But that hadn't been the way it had happened.

He had to go inside again.

*

The first thing that had surprised all six kids as they'd entered the building was the smell. Without even thinking of it, they'd all expected to be hit with the blood-and-sawdust odour of the butcher's. But it wasn't like that at all. Apart from the faintest whiff of uncleaned cages, the pervasive smell was that of old hospitals – carbolic and chloroform, as if the institute had been designed to help make the animals get better.

Adam knew better. More than ever before, he wished he could shut Mammalogue out. His head was filled with an agonized tumult of suffering. Instinctively, he put his hands to his ears, but nothing could silence the voices.

"This way," Terry called, and the others chased after him.

They ran down a long, lino-covered corridor, through swing doors and into a huge central laboratory. It was a high-ceilinged hall, lined with rows of stacked cages. As the realization of where they were struck them, they all stopped. They had reached their goal and suddenly were at a loss to know what to do next. Gradually the entire picture became all too vividly clear. Dexter and Denise burst into tears. Terry roared furiously.

Adam remained calm.

It was worse than he could ever have imagined.

He picked up two smooth pebbles and rubbed them slowly together. Memories! He chucked them back into the waves, where they disappeared without a trace. His hair was being blown about in the wind while below him, in the murky water, the strands of seaweed were being tossed around in just the same way.

The worst of it was realizing that during all those years of listening to the distant voices of countless animals, part of what he could hear had been the sound of those poor, lost creatures at the institute.

And he hadn't known.

"Vic!" he heard Terry shouting. "Vic, boy!" And he had started to clip through the wire to let his dog out of the padlocked cage.

They were all there: all the pets that were missing from the town, as well as countless others that had been bred or imported to be used in the various experiments being carried out at the institute.

"Smoke," Naima screamed.

She'd found the cat, but she was in no state to be taken home. She lay still and unseeing on the floor of her cage, a thick plaster stuck to her head.

Adam wandered round the hall in a daze. He opened the doors that lead into smaller rooms off the main laboratory. Clearly, there were several kinds of research being carried out. Some of the animals had been drugged up and were cowering in the corners of their cages. Others had been strapped into fixed positions to stop them scratching away the chemicals being tested on their skin or in their eyes. One room was full of monkeys and apes that looked so ill, he knew they must have been injected with various diseases. It occurred to him that if *they* escaped, they could spread the illnesses to any animals or people they came into contact with. He ran back to the main hall to warn the others not to let the animals go.

But it was too late.

All five of them were running around from cage to cage, releasing the catches and letting the doors swing open.

"Don't!" Adam called.

None of them heard him.

He shrugged. It was too bad. If any of the germs spread beyond the institute, it was the scientists' fault for infecting healthy animals in the first place.

We're not to blame, he thought, and joined in with the others, unlocking the cages.

"WHAT ON EARTH DO YOU THINK YOU'RE DOING?"

The six kids had been so intent on their mission of setting free every single imprisoned animal that none of them had noticed the door at the far end of the laboratory opening. It was only as the deep, booming voice echoed round the hall that they looked up.

There in the doorway, silhouetted against a dazzlingly bright light behind him, was the figure of a thin, gaunt man with wild hair. His elongated shadow stretched out in front of him, running the length of the laboratory's central aisle.

For an instant there was silence.

The children stared in horror at the man; the animals cowered in their cages.

Then, as if to some pre-arranged signal, everything sprang into frantic action. The kids scattered in all directions to take cover behind the cages. The dogs began barking and skidded away across the shiny lino. Rats and mice leapt down from their cages and scampered towards the light pouring in through the open door. While the monkeys climbed up to the top of the rows of cages and screeched in alarm as the man strode down into the hall.

Adam had crawled under the cages and was backing down a row parallel to the central aisle. As he walked along, he continued to flick the catches open, and watched as the multitude of animals came tumbling out of their cages. Cautiously retreating, taking care not to tread on any of the freed rodents, he aimed to where he thought the exit was.

"Come on!" he could hear Terry and Naima calling him from the door. "Hurry up!"

He kept moving backwards, his heart beating furiously.

Nearly there, nearly there, he urged himself.

"WATCH OUT!" he heard Denise screaming and an instant later, he was grabbed from behind.

"Help!" he yelled out, and bit into the scientist's hand.

The man cursed violently under his breath but didn't release his grip.

Adam knew he was done for. The man was much too strong for him and he couldn't get free, however much he kicked and struggled. There was only one last hope. Mammalogue.

'HELP!' he thought. 'HELP ME!'

The hands released their grip instantly.

'RUN, ADAM,' a thousand voices commanded him.

And he did so, not daring to turn around until he had reached the far end of the narrow passageway between the stacks of cages. From his point of safety, he stopped and looked back. The man had his arms up and was tugging away at two monkeys that had jumped down on to his head and were wrenching his hair out in thick clumps.

"G . . . arrggh . . ." he was yelling indistinctly.

Finally managing to rid himself of the monkeys, he hurled them away and looked down the rows at the boy. His and Adam's eyes met.

"No," Adam murmured, as the man rushed headlong at him.

He got two steps and no further. Two cats darted out in front of him from under the cages, tripping him up and sending him sprawling through the air, arms wheeling frantically as he tried to regain his balance. He landed with a crashing thud, his head knocking viciously against one of the steel cage doors and bouncing back heavily on to the floor.

Adam couldn't move. He stood there, staring down at the motionless body on the floor without so much as blinking. A thin trickle of blood emerged from near the man's ear.

The silence of the animals gave way to the sound of sirens wailing outside and the laboratory was illuminated with a pulsing blue light. Adam watched as Terry approached the body. All his movements seemed to be impossibly slow as the light continued to flash. He saw him crouch down and reach his hand out.

"I think he's dead."

He's dead.

He's dead.

He's dead.

The words repeated over and over as the waves crashed against the jetty. Time and again, the swell of the sea would build up and send a volley of foam, pebbles and sand hurtling at the concrete. Whoosh, it went. Whoosh. And Adam was suddenly back in his own distant past – sitting on a bus, copying the noise of the doors, which in turn were copying the sounds in his head. The sounds he could hear now.

Sitting in the same place every day, the weeks had drifted into months. It was seldom that his recollections of the incident in the laboratory got so far. Usually, he would stop at the door – his memory protecting him from what had followed. But today was an unusual day. He had gone back into the building and had relived the horror of the animals' pain, the thrill of unlocking their cages, the fear of being captured.

The sun was now low in the sky, shining down on the sea over by the horizon. Above him, the dark clouds dimmed the entire scene, turning the late afternoon blue. A deep, shimmering blue, pulsating as Adam stared at the breakers crashing against the sea-wall. And with the conditions around him, blue, flashing, so reminiscent of the night in the laboratory, his memory took him back there for the first time since the incident had taken place.

"Dear, oh dear!" voices exclaimed as the policemen walked into the institute.

"What a mess!"

The police had been alerted by a neighbour, who had heard the row going on from a quarter of a mile away. They found the guards tied up outside, but the German shepherds wouldn't let anyone near them. Although they had taken orders from a new master, their obedience had remained complete.

Inside, the policemen were confronted with a scene like a hideous mockery of the Ark. There were hundreds of animals, limping, crawling, diseased. Some were bandaged, some blinded, some were bearing broad areas of raw skin where their fur had been shaved away. The fittest of them made a sudden dash for the exit. The weakest hadn't even left their unlocked cages. The four kids by the door offered no resistance – two boys, two girls; they stood there, dazed and motionless. In one of the narrow aisles between the countless rows of cages, two more boys were kneeling down beside a body.

"Come on, you lot," one of the policemen had said, and they began to steer the young trespassers outside to the waiting cars.

None of them was charged. In fact, once the story broke the following day, they became temporary heroes. Five of them woke up to find their photos on the front of all the national papers. The incident led to a full, independent investigation into the Dimwell Institute. This developed into a separate inquiry into the rest of the country's research laboratories. And when the committee's findings were finally published two years later, the report was so harshly critical that it led to a radical change in the law concerning the use of laboratory animals.

The only face not present in the group photographs had been Adam's. He hadn't been up to it.

When the policeman had come to take him away to the car, he had remained rigidly staring down at the dead body, as if the continuing flashing blue light had hypnotized him.

"Come on, son," the policeman had said.

But Adam had made no move.

"Did you know him?" he'd asked.

Adam had looked up tearfully then. He shook his head. No, he didn't know him. He couldn't know him, could he?

But today, with the eerie blue light of the impending storm wrapped around the harbour, Adam was right back there once more. The waves crashed into the concrete below him, sending the foam spraying up into his face.

Of course he knew who he was.

The dead scientist lying on the floor beside him was his father.

Adam stood up and yelled out as loud as he could into the stormy wind.

"MY FATHER. MY FATHER! MY FATHER!!"

And with those two words, repeated over and over, he felt he had suddenly been allowed to leave the nightmare that had been haunting him all these months. Because the words didn't mean 'my father is dead', they meant 'my father was responsible for all that pain'.

It was something he hadn't been able to accept. Something he had tried to reject, even to the point of shutting out the entire world – to the point of denying Mammalogue. How could he communicate with animals when *he* knew and *they* knew that his own father had overseen all those horrendous experiments, with all the suffering they had involved. Ashamed and guilty, he had cut himself off from the animals; refusing to talk and pretending not to hear.

Until now.

With the memory of the night at the institute suddenly back in its horrifying entirety, Adam had been released from his self-imposed prison. He hadn't wanted to admit that his father had been responsible, but now that he had, the misplaced shame and guilt had been removed from his own shoulders.

'It wasn't my fault!' he yelled out. 'I'm sorry for everything that took place, but I wasn't to blame!'

At that moment there was a flurry of movement below the water and a huge, sleek dolphin leapt out into the air, performed a perfect somersault and dived back into the foaming waves.

'If you'd only listened,' Adam heard in his head, 'that's what I've been trying to tell you for months.'

He looked round and the animal burst through the surface of the sea again and spun gracefully through the air.

'Jump in,' it cried.

'It's dangerous,' Adam thought back.

'This? Dangerous? After all you've been through?'

Adam laughed, stripped off his clothes and took a running leap from the jetty. Immediately he landed in the cold, deep water, he felt the dolphin nosing him back up to the surface. He reached round its smooth, warm body and held on to the dorsal fin.

'All set?' the dolphin asked.

'I think so,' Adam replied, checking his grip.

'We're off!'

And with that, the dolphin kicked its tail heavily down and the two of them sped off out to sea.

'We thought we'd lost you for ever,' the dolphin thought, turning round. 'Welcome back!'

—16—
THE DOLPHIN'S TALE

Of all the animals in the world to be welcomed back to Mammalogue by, the dolphins were undoubtedly the best. And of all the dolphins in the oceans of the world, Adam was convinced that Iko was the most wonderful individual he could possibly have met. Every morning he would get up as soon as the sky began to brighten and race down to the beach. Standing at the end of the jetty, he would call out the dolphin's name.

"Eeee–kooooo."

The two syllables would echo over the sea and in a matter of minutes, the dolphin had appeared in front of him, chattering and clicking excitedly. At twelve foot long, Iko was more than twice as big as Adam, and whenever the boy jumped into the water, the sheer size of his companion made him feel apprehensive for a moment. He would remember that dolphins could kill sharks, and if they chose to, could certainly break a boy's spine with a single head butt. But the huge smile playing round the dolphin's mouth calmed any panic.

'Where to today?' Iko would ask.

'Your choice,' Adam would reply, and they would race off to nearby islands, floating rafts of seaweed, solitary rocks. Or when the weather was safe, Iko would set a straight course for Ireland or France.

As the weather grew colder at the end of another summer, Miriam bought Adam a wet-suit and a mask so that he wouldn't catch pneumonia out in the water. She worried, of course, about him disappearing for so many hours at a time. But the change in Adam's behaviour since meeting the dolphin had been even more marked than when she had introduced Oscar to the toddler. She was not about to interfere.

'What's this?' Iko asked, as he rubbed against the curious rubber layer for the first time.

'Wet-suit,' Adam explained. 'It keeps me warm.'

Iko examined it further; circling the boy and looking him up and down with his big eyes.

'It'll do,' he thought at length.

Adam smiled. Anything that humans fashioned for the water was necessarily second-best. Iko's skin felt quite unique. Unlike his own dry skin, it was covered with an oily substance which was soft to the touch but not slimy. As the pair of them skimmed across the water, rising and falling, Adam's hold on the dolphin's fin never slipped, while the smoothness of his skin helped Iko to propel the pair of them effortlessly through the deep sea.

Unlike all the other animals that he'd ever come across, Adam felt that he was really getting to know Iko. Even with Oscar, he'd always remained aware that although they could communicate, the pair of them were very different.

With the dolphin, that difference disappeared, and he soon discovered so much about his new companion's character. Iko, like all the other dolphins he met, was kind, humorous, patient, gentle. They were everything he liked about his friends, but had none of the traits he hated in obnoxious people. Among the dolphins, there seemed to be no equivalent of the Lawrence-Wilson-bully-boy aggression that Adam had come across at school.

'We learnt a long, long time ago that unnecessary violence is counter-productive,' Iko explained.

'What do you mean?'

'Well, violence should only be used in a dangerous situation — like when you're being attacked by a shark. But if it's used just to prove you're bigger and stronger, then the person you attack will retaliate — or, worse than that, take it out on someone weaker ... No, it's pointless. It's bad for the species,' he added. 'Dolphins don't have wars.'

Every evening Adam would return to his aunt's cottage with something else to think about. Dolphins don't have wars. Dolphins sing but they can't shout. While humans work, dolphins play. Dolphins have no money as there's nothing any of them want. Dolphins don't write, so every one of them has memorized the entire history of the species.

In fact, as Adam learnt more and more about his friend, he found that there was one important difference between them after all. Iko was far more intelligent. When they met up with other dolphins out at sea Adam noticed how fast they communicated, and it occurred to him that when speaking with the boy, Iko had to slow himself down and deliberately simplify everything. He knew from his old encyclopaedia that dolphins had larger brains than humans, but nevertheless, it came as a shock to be confronted with creatures so intellectually superior.

'It isn't just the size of the brain,' Iko told him. 'Humans only use about ten per cent of their thinking potential, whereas way, way back we learnt that a minimum of seventy per cent use was necessary for the smooth running of the species.'

'But what do you *do* with all that extra thinking?' Adam asked, bewildered by the idea of being able to use his brain more than he already did.

'Oh, a thousand things,' Iko replied. 'For a start, we can "see" sounds.'

'How?'

'Easy,' the dolphin replied. 'Get ready for a long dive and I'll show you.'

Once down in the milky-green water, the dolphin began his familiar high-pitched clicking sound. Turning this way and that, he finally detected a silver-white fish.

'Now close your eyes,' Iko instructed, 'and I'll show you what I can see.'

Adam did as he was told. Rather than being plunged into darkness, everything turned a dim blue-green. Ahead of him he could see a beam of tiny lines pouring out of Iko's head and away into the distance. They locked on to the fish and bounced back towards his lower jaw. On receiving the returning set of echoes, the dolphin flicked his tail down and sped off towards the fish. As they got closer, Adam saw how the sound seemed to penetrate the fish, showing the bones and swim-bladder like an X-ray. A moment later and Iko caught it in his mouth and the pair of them returned to the surface.

'That was wonderful,' Adam thought.

'I believe human scientists have developed a similar, though far more primitive system for their hospitals,' Iko thought back as he swallowed the last of the fish. 'We've been able to do that for millions of years.'

'What else can you do?' Adam asked excitedly.

'Well, there's magnetic map-reading,' Iko suggested non-chalantly.

'What's that?' he asked. 'No, don't tell me, show me.'

Iko swam out a little further to where the current from a nearby river passed. It had been raining recently and it was almost impossible to see through the silty water.

'Have you got your breath back?'

'Yup,' Adam replied.

They dived again. At first Adam looked around him, but even through the mask, he was unable to see further than a couple of metres. Iko told him to close his eyes again, and when he did so, the view that greeted Adam this time was entirely different. Down in the murky depths he suddenly found he could see a range of hills and valleys disappearing into the distance.

'But what are they?'

'Magnetic landmarks,' Iko told him. 'This is what the slight variations in the strength of the earth's magnetic field looks like. And we follow them,' he added then, diving down into a deep valley and swimming along the bottom. 'It's just the same as humans using the contours of the countryside to find their way about.'

Back at the surface, Adam breathed deep.

'So, it's like a huge underwater map,' he thought.

'Precisely,' Iko replied. 'The difference is that you have to carry a map of each region with you. We have a chart of the entire ocean in our head.'

Adam didn't know what to say. He'd always assumed that as dolphins hadn't got any hands, they were at something of a disadvantage. Being with Iko, he was slowly coming to the conclusion that it was precisely *because* of their hands that humans' brains had stopped growing.

'And then there's music,' the dolphin continued.

'But we have music.'

'Ah, but not like this. Not so varied.'

'But it must be,' he argued. 'There's pop and heavy metal and jazz and classical and . . . and country and western.'

'Ssshhh,' Iko thought back. 'Be quiet and listen.'

They slipped back down below the waves and Adam did as he was told. At first all he could hear was the sound of the waves above him and the sand shifting below his feet. But slowly, as he ignored those sounds and listened beyond, he heard something else. Something infinitely more beautiful and melodic and varied than anything he had ever heard on the radio. It was the song of the sea.

'But . . .' he started to think.

'Listen,' Iko repeated.

And as he continued to listen to the tunes streaming in from near and far, enfolding him in their succession of notes, he felt that he was being included in the music. This was what he had been able to hear in the distant background ever since he was born. Now, for the first time, he realized that the music wasn't simply something separate for him to listen to. Adam himself was actually a part of it.

By the time Iko took him back to the surface, he had almost forgotten that he wasn't able to breathe underwater. It'd felt so comfortable and secure where he was.

'That's what I could hear,' he thought. 'All those years.'

'I know,' Iko replied.

Something occurred to Adam. He had almost given up hoping that any animal could answer his question about Mammalogue, but the dolphin had seemed so positive about the music that perhaps it was worth one more try. And yet he'd been disappointed before.

'Do you know . . .' he hesitated and, frightened of having this last hope dashed, changed the question. 'Do you know what 98,452 divided by 213 is?'

'462.21596. Why?' the dolphin replied instantly.

'And what about 29 per cent of 367?'

'106.43.'

'What day was the fourth of June 1955?'

'On your calendar, a Saturday. What's this all about?' Iko asked him mischievously. 'I rather get the impression you're not asking me the question you want to ask.'

Adam looked away, embarrassed. They were near the shore and he slid down from the dolphin's back on to the hard, rippled sand.

'Well,' Iko thought to the boy, 'it's getting dark. I'll see you to . . .'

Adam turned round and looked the dolphin straight in the eye.

'Do you know why I speak Mammalogue?' he finally managed to blurt out.

'Yes,' Iko replied simply. 'Yes, I do.'

Miriam had decided to take her son away from the town he'd grown up in, despite the family doctor's advice. Having seen the boy improve over the years from what had initially been diagnosed as autism, to a stage where he was able to attend the local comprehensive school and compete favourably with his contemporaries, he thought it better for Adam to come to terms with the situation in his home environment. Miriam's *mother's instinct*, however, nagged at her that this was the wrong decision. She knew that Adam had settled down in the new school. She knew that he'd made a lot of friends. On the other hand, she knew that he was blaming himself for his father's death, and nothing she could say could change the way he was feeling. Oscar could have managed it, but Oscar was no longer there. And she would always remain a poor substitute.

The only thing which might have persuaded her to stay

was the zoo. Adam had loved his weekend visits to the animals, but since the incident at Dimwell's, he hadn't seemed to want to return there. She would suggest it occasionally, only to be greeted by a sullen silence. Knowing how well he had got on with Tom Hutchinson, the keeper, she had phoned him for his opinion. He had only confirmed what she herself thought: if he didn't want to go to the zoo for the time being, there was no point in forcing him.

"It's a shame though," he added. "We're having a massive extension built. Still, he can see it when he's better."

"I'll stay in touch," Miriam had promised.

Her mind was made up. It was bad enough for *her*, having to remain in the house with its mix of good and bad memories. For Adam, it was evidently intolerable. She had contacted her sister who lived down on the north Cornwall coast on the Friday evening and by the Sunday morning they were packed up and ready to go.

Adam hardly registered the move. At least, not outwardly. Perhaps he was taking it all in, but nothing showed.

"It's a lovely room, isn't it?" his mother was saying with artificial jollity, as she drew the curtains and helped him shift his clothes from suitcase and holdall to wardrobe and drawers. "And *look* at the view."

There were a couple of slate roofs below him, and beyond that the harbour with its jetty, nets, lobster pots and assortment of colourful fishing-boats bobbing about on the high tide. The sun was setting far away to the west. Adam looked, without really seeing, and returned to his Ark, which he was arranging in the corner. The animals were all trooping on board, two by two, up the gangplank. The pieces were made of heavy wood, and when he'd been packing it up, Miriam had asked whether he wasn't a bit too old for it now, whether it wouldn't be better to leave it until they came back. The look of panic and hatred that had instantly come over his face persuaded her otherwise.

And there, in his new room, with the wooden animals and the Ark spread out in front of him, Adam relived the trips he'd had with the animals he'd got to know so well.

You, he thought to the giraffes, you gave me the best view possible of the African plains. And he remembered how Lopa had carried him across the plains on her back to watch the migrating wildebeest.

And you told me why you have spots, and claws that don't retract, he added, as the two wooden cheetahs in his hand became his old zoo friends, Juba and Nyx.

Then there were Cuta and Roc, the horrible hyenas. They'd taken the mickey out of him because of his ears. And then they'd terrified him by leaving him on his own in the middle of the plains. Though if they hadn't, he might never have met Tom Hutchinson.

And Cana the elephant. Saty the chimpanzee and Mari the polar bear, and their babies Pan and Timus.

All the many, many animals who had taken Adam back with them into their memories of their past, where they were hunted and captured, their relatives killed, their home-lands destroyed.

Miriam watched her son as he picked up the animals in turn and placed them carefully around the Ark. There were tears in his eyes. But when she crouched down beside him to try and comfort him, Adam pulled away silently and turned his back to her.

How much longer? she wondered as she got up.

"Night, night, Adam," she whispered from the door.

He didn't reply.

As the weeks passed into months and he still remained locked into his own miserable private world, she began to wonder whether the previous ten years had really happened.

Had she deluded herself that her son had improved for an entire decade? Was wishful thinking really that strong? It was only by looking at the photographs she had taken of him as he'd been growing up that she knew it had actually happened. Those early days at St Jude's – she'd even taken a photograph of the poem he'd done about his first day; making sure Oscar took her tablets after one of her many accidents; cycling down the road on his new bike. It *had* all happened. And comparing that with the unresponsive boy he had become again, content to stare out at the horizon for hours on end, made it all the harder for Miriam to accept.

The day he came racing back from the harbour, soaking wet and ranting about someone or something called Iku or Echo, she had hardly allowed herself to believe it. And the following morning, she and her sister had looked at each other warily as Adam had continued to babble on about his trip out to sea with the dolphin.

"I knew it would be some animal or other that would bring him out of it," Miriam said, as he ran back down to the jetty.

"But it doesn't make any sense," Lucy had said.

Miriam just laughed.

"So what!"

If Adam hadn't spent so many months getting to know Iko, he would never have trusted his answer now. *Yes, I do*, the dolphin had replied to his question about Mammalogue and Adam believed him. And yet, all the same, it was incredible. All those years he'd spent trying to find out why he had been born with the gift, or curse, as he'd often considered it, of Mammalogue. The hedgehog, the bear, the elephant, the cheetahs, the hyenas – none of them had been able to tell him why. Even Oscar hadn't known why he should have been singled out.

Iko the dolphin, however, apparently did know.

'Why then?' he asked, trying to remain calm.

'Easy,' he said. 'Because we wanted you to.'

Adam thought he must have misheard the dolphin — even though he knew that in Mammalogue, mistakes of communication never happened.

'But why? And when? And who's *we* anyway?' Adam demanded.

'Well, to take it in reverse order,' Iko said. '*We* are the cetaceans — the dolphins and the whales.'

'The ocean mammals,' Adam said.

'Yes, but there are some of us living in rivers too: the Indus, the Ganges, the Yangtze, the Amazon . . .'

'And?' Adam interrupted him impatiently.

'When? Well, that was all to do with the numbers. The positions of the stars, the angle of the wind, the frequency of the waves, the strength of the current, the state of the tides — we had to calculate all of this mathematically — and then the figure we arrived at indicated the time and date and places of birth for those we needed. It took so . . .'

'Yes, yes, yes,' Adam urged him. 'And why? Why?'

'That,' Iko answered, 'will take me longer to explain. I know you've waited a long time, but if you remain patient a while longer, I'll tell you everything. Hey, Adam,' he added, 'you are listening to me, aren't you? This is important.'

Adam turned round and looked at Iko. His smiley face was still bobbing around just off the shoreline. He realized that he hadn't even been looking at the dolphin. He had been busy pacing back and forwards, head down, irritably kicking the foaming waves as they tumbled on to the beach. Why didn't the stupid animal just get on with it and tell him? Why was he burbling on about being patient? Patient? He'd been waiting long enough, hadn't he? Now what was the hold-up? All that stuff about numbers.

Numbers, Adam thought. What had he been saying about numbers? And it occurred to him that he really hadn't been listening at all.

'I'm sorry.'

'It's understandable,' Iko replied. 'Come and sit down at the water's edge and I'll explain.'

Adam waded in up to his knees and sat down in the foamy water. Iko flicked his tail and swam nearer, stopping with his head resting on the boy's legs. Adam leant back on one hand and stroked the animal's soft skin with the other.

'This is how it all began,' Iko thought. 'On the edge of a prehistoric sea some thirty million years ago.'

'Do we need to go back *that* far?' Adam asked, alarmed at just how long the story was going to take.

'I think we should,' Iko thought back.

And he started to tell his tale to Adam about how his ancestors had originally wandered the continental plains with the other animals, balancing the need for food with the desire not to be eaten. Of course, they'd had legs then, and though they were a little cumbersome on land, they had managed well enough. And yet a certain lack of aggression forced them to retreat if other animals challenged their territory.

Gradually, as time passed, they were pushed back to the coastal areas and waded into the swampy mud, foraging for food. Apparently, they looked something like a cross between a carnivorous camel and a small hippopotamus. But even then, what singled them out from the rest of the animals was their intelligence. It occurred to them that with all the mammals of the world crammed together on the land, ninety per cent of the planet had been left for them to investigate. And it was with this thought that they forsook the land for ever.

Soon streamlining themselves for their new watery world,

the new species which developed evolved with no hair, no hind limbs and long sleek bodies which propelled them across the oceans. There were dangers, of course — giant octopus and squid, electric eels and rays, and bloodthirsty sharks. But none of the creatures of the sea was a match for the dolphins and whales. Instead of merely relying on their instincts, they could actually think their way out of trouble.

And it was in these cool, blue, untroubled waters that, in the same way a child plays with plastic toys, the dolphins and whales began to play with ideas. Their brains grew and grew and they became wiser and wiser.

'It was, in a way, the golden age, and we still recite poems and sing songs of those far-away distant days.'

Adam was still sitting in the shallow water. Iko's tale was fascinating him but, despite his wet-suit, he was getting cold.

'You've gone completely blue,' Iko noticed, as he broke off from his fond memories and looked up.

'I'm all right.'

'Well, you don't look it. I think we ought to postpone our story till tomorrow. I don't want you dying of pneumonia now.'

'Oh, go on,' Adam persisted.

'No,' Iko replied definitely, and Adam knew that there was no point in arguing. 'Be back here at seven tomorrow morning,' he added and, twisting round, he disappeared under the water.

Adam walked back to the cottage, his teeth continuing to chatter. It was frustrating to have got so far with the story, only to find that it had been broken off once again without reaching its conclusion. But at least he was now near to a guaranteed answer. And, if nothing else, the hours he had to wait would give him time to consider all he had already been told.

The fact that the dolphins and whales seemed to have some master plan that they were slowly putting into operation. The fact that he, Adam Williams, had been selected after some incredible mathematical calculation. The fact that the sea creatures were still passing down the tales that had been first told thirty million years earlier. It was all too much to take in.

"Good day?" Miriam asked when he got in.

"Mm hm."

"You were with your dolphin friend, were you?"

"Mmm."

"I tried to find you earlier, but you must have been out in the water."

"Mmm."

"Adam!"

"Yes?"

"I'm talking to you."

"I know, you tried to find me. What for?"

"That keeper at the zoo phoned up," she explained.

"Who, Tom?"

"That's the one. Tom Hutchinson. He said that there's a job going at the zoo — if you want it. Working with the animals."

"Oh," said Adam quietly.

"Is that all? I thought you'd be pleased."

"Well, it's . . ." He didn't want to tell his mother all about Iko's tale, but he knew he couldn't leave now. "It's just . . ." he started again.

"It doesn't matter anyway," she continued. "You couldn't start before your sixteenth birthday anyway, so you've got a couple of months to think about it. But I said you'd phone him back for a chat before the end of the week. OK?"

"OK," said Adam and smiled.

He realized suddenly how much he missed the Hutchinsons. They'd become his weekend family, his alternative family and, without noticing it, during the months he'd spent visiting the zoo, he'd grown really attached to them.

'I'll phone him on Saturday," he said. It would be nice to see them all again.

But not just yet.

—17—
ADAM'S ROLE

Adam hardly slept that night. Again and again his mind went over the story that Iko had begun to tell him and his imagination kept trying to work out how it would all end. Occasionally, he would drop off to sleep. But it was light, troubled and full of dreams of four-legged whales lumbering across deserts; humpbacks, hundreds of miles apart, singing to one another down deep-sea telephone lines; dolphins bouncing around in the foaming waves, heading a huge, football-sized brain back and forwards between them. And now and then, the sound of a single, plaintively calling dolphin would drag him from his dreams.

Lying awake in the darkness, however, listening to the familiar, distant voices, he was unable to tell what had woken him. He climbed out of bed and looked out at the moon glittering on the sea.

If only the sun would hurry up and rise, he thought impatiently.

But everything takes its time and neither the sun nor the moon, the tides nor even a dolphin's story can be hurried. He climbed back into bed and was surprised to be woken up by the alarm clock what seemed like a couple of minutes later.

At last!

Standing back down on the jetty in his wet-suit and flippers a few minutes later, he scanned the calm sea for any trace of Iko.

Surely it must be seven o'clock by now, he thought nervously, and imagined all sorts of disasters that might have occurred to the dolphin in the night. He could have got caught up in tuna nets, or eaten a contaminated fish, or electrocuted himself on a bare underground cable. There were so many dangers under the water now that hadn't been there when their ancestors had first returned to the sea.

The church bell in the village rang and as it chimed seven, Iko burst out of the water, did a double-somersault and splashed back down again.

'How do you always time everything so well?' Adam asked.

'It's just something else we cetaceans can do,' Iko replied. 'Time is a rhythmic pattern, like music, like mathematics — we are simply in tune with it.'

Adam shook his head in amazement. There didn't seem to be any end to the animals' abilities.

'Come on then,' Iko called out. 'Jump in and grab hold. We don't want to be interrupted.'

Adam whooped with child-like joy as they sped off across the water again. He clung hold of the fin of the living torpedo below him and from his elevated position, he looked down as they carved a way through the waves, leaving a trail of foam in their wake. Near a rock, just beyond the horizon, Iko slowed down and let Adam slip off his back.

'I don't think we'll be disturbed here,' Iko thought matter-of-factly. 'Now, where were we?'

'In the cool, blue, untroubled waters becoming wiser and wiser,' Adam answered as promptly and accurately as he could.

Iko smiled.

'So we were. For millions of years this went on, until the appearance of humans.'

Adam swallowed nervously, wondering what the dolphin was going to say.

'When we first noticed them leaving the trees, getting together in groups, learning to use tools, we never gave it that much thought. We just assumed they were slightly cleverer than average apes. But then, about 100,000 years ago, definite signs of intelligence began to appear. A drop in the ocean, so to speak, compared with how long we've been around, but once the process had begun, it increased at a phenomenal rate.'

'You mean human intelligence?'

'Yes,' Iko thought back. 'There are some who believe that humans are quite simply insane — but perhaps it was just circumstances that made them what they are.'

'Circumstances?' Adam asked.

'Well, take a human worker. What does he do? Spends his whole life struggling to provide food, shelter and transport for himself and his family. He works to earn money, to pay for the food produced by farmers, the energy dug out of the ground by miners, to buy clothes, houses, machines. Every minute is used up trying to tame, to control, to govern his environment. It's completely the opposite to what we dolphins and whales have done.

'We've adapted to our surroundings. Food is no problem. We don't need houses, so there are no problems with ghettos and slums. We don't have any possessions, so greediness doesn't exist. And we don't claim to own special areas of the sea, so we never invented atomic bombs or nerve gases or defoliants or machine-guns or barbed wire or any of the other horrors of war humans need to defend their patches of land.'

It all sounded so depressing. Adam turned away miserably.

'Cheer up,' Iko added, 'it's still not too late.'

'Isn't it?'

'Certainly not. There's still a little time left, and that's where you come in.'

Adam remained unconvinced.

'From the earliest times,' Iko continued, 'it became obvious what humans would do with the environment. They were busy chopping down forests, conquering the mountains, destroying the grass plains without a thought for the future. In contrast, we couldn't *stop* thinking about the future – and that proved to be just as dangerous. If humans act too quickly and thoughtlessly, we cetaceans think so much we never seem to get anything done. But then, on the other hand, it's so easy to make mistakes.'

'What? You mean dolphins make mistakes too?' Adam asked.

'On the odd occasion,' Iko admitted, a little defensively. 'We thought that as man was gradually taking over every corner of the land, the only option open to the other land mammals was to follow our example and take to the sea. Unfortunately, we carried out all the early experiments far too quickly and the result was disastrous.'

Iko fell silent, and turned to face Adam. For a dolphin, he looked remarkably sheepish.

'So what happened?'

'Well, we tried it out on one particular species first. Just to see if it would work. We implanted the desire to return to the sea in their heads and waited to see what would happen.'

'Well?'

'Well, it worked – I mean, millions of them suddenly upped and left the land. They leapt into the sea and set off. Unfortunately, although we'd given them the will to live in the sea, evolution hadn't equipped them with either the gills or flippers. And they drowned. All of them. And it happened again and again. We couldn't seem to get them to break the habit.'

'These animals,' Adam asked slowly, 'they wouldn't be lemmings, would they?'

'I believe that's what humans call them,' Iko answered, looking away.

'So *you* were responsible for that, were you?' Adam thought. 'I've often wondered.'

'You'd have thought by now they'd have at least learnt to hold their breath,' Iko thought peevishly. 'Anyway, you can see the enormous responsibility we realized we had.'

Adam nodded.

'The trouble is, time's running out. The human population of the world has increased from one billion to six billion over the last two hundred years. If you look at all the living creatures on earth, one species is becoming extinct every single hour. And it's not just because they're being hunted. The land, the water, the air; it's all being poisoned so rapidly that if we don't act fast, there won't be anywhere left capable of supporting life. This sea, for instance, is filthy.'

'But it doesn't look that bad,' Adam thought.

'It never does,' Iko agreed. 'The fish that killed my wife

and son didn't *look* as though it was full of deadly levels of cadmium and mercury.'

'You mean . . .' Adam started. Iko had never spoken of his family before, and the boy had just assumed his friend was a bit of a loner. Hearing that the dolphin, just like all the other animals he'd ever met, had had his own personal tragedy made Adam feel especially sad – particularly as he had mentioned it almost in passing.

It obviously still hurt him to talk about it.

'So we had to step up our experiments,' Iko went on. 'We used the American navy a lot at first. They were so *stupid*! They'd stick these discs and cylinders into the water and we'd have to say which was which. Not too hard, that one,' he noted sarcastically. 'Then they'd try to trick us by putting in different metals: aluminium, brass, copper, steel and get us to differentiate them.'

'No problem at all to an animal that can X-ray fish with sound waves, I'd have thought,' Adam suggested.

'Precisely. But the games continued. They didn't realize that it was *us* experimenting on *them*. We gave them the idea that we might be useful for attaching mines on to enemy ships, and they duly tried it out. Nine times out of ten we did what they wanted us to do, then the tenth time we'd return with the mine and stick it on the side of their own hull. It caused pandemonium.'

Adam laughed at the idea of the sailors panicking as they watched the dolphin they thought they'd trained, returning with the deadly explosive device.

'Time after time they tried it, and in the end gave up because they thought we were too erratic to trust. What they didn't know, because they *would not* listen, was that we were trying to show them how moronic warfare itself was. Hopeless! So, having given up on the armed forces, we tried experiments on the ordinary public.'

'How did you manage that?' Adam asked.

'Oh, through leisure parks, dolphinariums, that sort of thing.'

Adam stared at Iko in amazement. It had never for an instant occurred to him that all the while humans thought they were experimenting on dolphins, the truth was the exact reverse.

'That was as it should be,' Iko explained. 'If a subject *knows* it is being examined, the results of the test are always artificial.'

'And what did you discover?'

'Well, at first it was disastrous. They would think that they'd bribed us to turn somersaults, retrieve balls, leap through hoops and so on with the promise of a fish, but their minds would remain closed to us. It seemed as though humans had isolated themselves from the animal kingdom to such an extent that we could have no useful influence on them. It was much later that we stumbled on the solution.

'A so-called dolphin expert in New Zealand claimed he could train us by telepathy. He was right, of course, although it wasn't really training. We were just trying to show him that we could hear him when he thought to us. Sadly, *he* still couldn't hear *us*. We realized that the only way we were ever going to communicate with humans properly was by Mammalogue. And as man had lost the ability to use the language, it meant we had to teach it to the baby before it was born.'

'But how?'

'It wasn't easy,' Iko admitted. 'As the human develops from conception to birth, he or she goes through all the stages of evolution. A period with gills, a period with a tail, a period when Mammalogue is possible.'

Adam remembered the conversations he'd had with Tom's baby son, Roland. Before he'd learned to tune in to the human language, they'd been able to chat away quite happily in Mammalogue. But the ability had soon faded away.

'And as I said before,' Iko was continuing, 'it took incredibly complicated mathematics to determine who should be picked and when. Split-second timing was essential.'

'And that baby was me?'

'Well, you were one of them,' Iko thought back.

Adam stared at him.

'You mean there are others?'

'In different parts of the world, yes. One person wasn't enough for the task that lies ahead.'

'The task ahead . . .' Adam repeated dully.

His head was beginning to reel. All the assumptions he had been making all his life were crumbling. Humans *weren't* the most intelligent creatures on the planet. He *hadn't* instinctively understood Mammalogue, he had been taught it. And now he had discovered that he *wasn't* the only human on earth that could communicate with mammals the way he did.

'And now?' Adam asked.

'Now comes the hardest part of all,' Iko replied. 'We are going to run an Ark.'

'AN ARK!' the boy exclaimed. 'You mean like with Noah?'

'Not quite. Noah's Ark was only a myth. This time, it's going to be for real.'

'But it's in all the old religions, from all over the world,' Adam protested, remembering the project he'd done all those years ago. 'It can't just be a story.'

'Dolphins are all over the world,' Iko explained patiently. 'We thought up the story and gave it to humans some six thousand years ago. It was passed on by word of mouth down the centuries. Of course, unlike *our* tales which remain word-perfect, it changed a lot in the telling, but the main idea remained. We had to give humans the story — to whet their appetite, as it were — so that now we really need an Ark or two, the idea doesn't seem too strange.'

But to Adam it did sound strange — it sounded ridiculous, crazy. It was all very well the dolphins claiming that humans were insane, but the idea of one almost-sixteen-year-old boy building an Ark for all the mammals of the world was the most stupid idea he'd ever heard.

'But . . . but, how big would they have to be?' he asked.

'Oh, many square miles in area,' Iko replied calmly.

'*I* can't build anything that size,' he protested.

'Of course you can't,' Iko thought back. 'No one's asking you to build anything. The Arks have all been built already.'

'They have?'

'Some of them still need some major improvements, but the basic structures are all there.'

Adam still didn't understand what the dolphin was getting at.

'Yes,' he continued, 'The Ark-building programme was started about a hundred and fifty years ago. But we found that on their own, they weren't sufficient. Assembling the animals in one place was easy enough, but they need looking after. They need caring for, nurturing and encouraging in their exile, by someone who can understand them, who can communicate with them, who can take care of them until that day when they can return to their original homes.'

As if someone had turned the light on in a huge, dark room that he'd been fumbling around lost in, Adam suddenly realized what Iko was referring to. It was the word Ark which had thrown him.

But then wasn't that, after all, what zoos were.

'And I am to take control of the zoo?' Adam asked.

Iko nodded gravely.

'For obvious reasons, *we* cannot now leave the sea. So it is up to you, Adam. You were selected to be a modern-day Noah, and now the time has come for you to assume that role.'

—18—
ABOARD THE ARK

"So the Australian section is on the other side, is it?" Miriam was asking.

"That's right," Adam replied. "With the areas for the Antarctic on the far side of that."

Since he had passed his driving-test, Adam had become increasingly independent of the other zoo-keepers. He had his own truck now and since ten o'clock that morning, he'd been driving his mother up and down the interlocking roadways, showing her everything he was responsible for.

The zoo was circular in shape and divided up into five different sections extending outwards from a central hill, which had been constructed to offer a view over the entire complex. The five segments coincided with the five main areas of the world, so that the animals of Africa, Asia, Australasia, America and Europe were kept in their microcosm of the continents they had originated from.

In addition, the zoo had been designed so that the warmest areas of the world were at the centre. Humid, tropical hot-houses, artificial deserts and subterranean buildings for the nocturnal animals were all situated around the central hill. Next, as the continental sections were subdivided into strips, roughly corresponding to the lines of latitude, came the Mediterranean regions. Further out, and areas of grassland representing the savannah, the steppes, the prairies of the different continents gave way to wooded enclosures with artificial streams, waterfalls and clearings. It was here in the temperate zone of the zoo that the bears, wolves, beavers, foxes, racoons and squirrels lived. And the sections continued outwards step by step to the polar regions, where giant refrigerating machinery re-created the appropriate conditions for the snow hares, seals, polar bears and penguins.

"It's all been terribly well designed," Miriam remarked.

"Hasn't it!" Adam said. "But I haven't shown you the best bit yet."

He continued to the end of the radial driveway and parked out on the perimeter road. Ahead of them was a wall with steps leading up to the top. It all looked rather like the battlements enclosing a medieval town.

"This is the newest part," Adam explained. "It was only finished just over a year ago."

"Uh huh," Miriam said, remembering the conversation she'd had with Tom Hutchinson on the phone all that time ago. He'd mentioned then that they were having a massive extension built. At that stage, Adam hadn't even begun to get over the shock of what had happened at Dimwell's. Miriam looked over at her son now as he led her across the road and up on to the wall. He had been a boy then. A frightened, lonely boy. In the three years since then, he had grown up.

As they reached the top of the ramparts and looked down on to the water below, the similarity between the zoo and a walled city became all the more striking. Stretching away from them, to the left and to the right, was a broad, deep moat.

"So what do you think?" Adam asked proudly.

"It's wonderful," Miriam said. "Wonderful."

Unlike an ordinary moat, however, the water was neither dark nor still, nor enclosed by grassy banks. Instead, it had been constructed as an ecologically functioning sea area.

"Incredible," Miriam added.

"It's just about as realistic as we could get it," Adam said, nodding.

A special generator created the waves while an automatic saline injector kept the level of the salt just right. Rather than painting the entire bottom turquoise the way zoos usually did with their pools, the zoo moat came with rocks, underwater caves and a shoreline which included sand, pebbles and mud-flats. It had initially been stocked with fish, sea weeds, turtles and various molluscs, and though the larger occupants of the pool still had to be given extra food, it had been calculated that within ten years it should become self-supporting. Waders, terns and oyster-catchers had already adopted the place as their home, and it was hoped that the pair of sea-eagles would nest there.

"And this goes right around the zoo, does it?" Miriam asked.

"Right round," Adam confirmed. "It's about thirty miles long altogether. Terry said that the only thing missing was an oil slick," he added and laughed.

"Terry?" Miriam repeated. "That's the boy you used to see over the park, isn't it?"

Adam nodded. "He works in a garage now," he said, "doing up write-offs. But he still drives over sometimes with the others — although I'm not sure whether they come to see me or . . . Hang on a minute.''

Adam looked up and down the moat. If they were right round the other side, they wouldn't be able to hear him. But he'd told them that he was bringing his mum along — no, they wouldn't let him down.

'Dol-phins,' he called out.

For a couple of seconds there was nothing. Then, just under the surface of the water, Adam saw a blur of movement and an instant later three dolphins broke the surface and somersaulted in front of them. They dived back into the water and then heaved themselves up on their tails and chattered greetings.

"Say hello," Adam told his mum.

"Hiya," she called out and waved.

"Aii-aa," the dolphins cried back, trying their best to imitate her voice, and fell back into the water.

"They're gorgeous," said Miriam.

As if determined to overwhelm their spectator totally, the three dolphins put on a spontaneous display of aquabatics which involved the most intricate of jumps, turns, dives and rolls, all in perfect sequence. At the end of it, Miriam could only applaud. Even Adam, who thought he'd seen just about everything, couldn't help but be impressed.

'Brilliant,' he thought.

'Well, we didn't want your mother to think we were a load of slackers, did we?' Iko replied.

'Clot,' Adam thought back affectionately.

'Come here and say that,' Iko responded, splashing about playfully.

'Later,' he promised, 'I'll come for a swim when the zoo's shut.'

Although at the time Adam hadn't had a clue how he was going to go about it, Iko had finally persuaded him to take over the running of a zoo. One nagging doubt had remained however. How would he know that he was doing everything correctly? Who would be there to confirm that he was taking the right decisions and making the right choices? What would happen if *his* zoo was no better than any of the others that existed?

When Iko had replied, 'but I'll be there with you, of course,' Adam had simply laughed. He thought he must have meant through Mammalogue, and it was only later that he realized the dolphin intended to be *really* with him.

On the Saturday, he'd phoned Tom Hutchinson up about the vacancy at the zoo, and it was then that he'd heard all about the opening of the new marine world. Tom had spoken at great length about the plans for the pool, detailing the various species of marine animals and plants which had been introduced to create a self-running ecosystem, and which could be observed from the overland walkway and underground viewing-chambers. Despite this, Adam hadn't been prepared for the sheer size of the project. He'd realized at once that this would be the ideal place for lonely Iko to live. Particularly as the water already contained an orphaned female called Anaka.

'But whenever you want to go back to the open sea,' Adam had explained to the dolphin when he had returned to the coast with the water-filled container-lorry, 'just tell me.'

'You didn't need to say that,' Iko replied. 'I trust you.'

That had been a little over a year ago. Since then, not only had three other dolphins opted for a new life in the inland Ark, helping Adam supervise the caring of the other mammals, but Iko and Anaka had evidently got together. As it doesn't show in dolphins, Adam hadn't even noticed that the female was pregnant. The first he knew was when he saw the tiny infant drinking the thick, rich milk from his mother's teat.

'It's a baby!' he'd exclaimed.

'Say hello to Adam,' Iko had instructed his baby son, and the tiny youngster had popped his head out of the water and clicked greetings.

'You can name him,' Iko had said.

'Are you sure?'

'Go ahead,' Iko had insisted. 'As an honorary dolphin, it's your right.'

'Well, what about Eeny?' Adam suggested, chuffed by the way they'd considered him. 'It was the name of Oscar's first kitten.'

'Eeny it is,' Anaka replied, and dived back down with her infant.

The infant dolphin was still only three weeks old, but in that time just about everyone Adam had ever known had come along to have a look. Prompted by his phone call, the teachers at St Jude's had organized the first trip to the zoo since they had brought Adam himself all those years ago. Mr Ashley had arranged day trips for his various biology classes. Terry, Dexter and Ian, Naima and Denise had all come along with friends of theirs to swap the latest news with Adam and to see the tiny new addition to the zoo. And now his mother had come up from the West Country for the weekend.

"He's absolutely fantastic," Miriam said. "Aren't you?" she added, clicking and cooing to the dolphin herself.

"Just think to him," Adam instructed. "He can understand you."

Miriam looked at her son, but didn't say anything. She returned her gaze to the family of dolphins.

"Anaka says 'thank you'," Adam said to his mother, "and added that, 'no, with all the dangers from pollution, fishing-nets and so on out in the sea, she's quite happy bringing little Eeny up here.'"

"How did you . . .?" she began.

But it wasn't worth pursuing. She had never really understood what went on between animals and her son. It had all been too disturbing; too painful at the time. And even now, when Adam seemed so content, the obvious communication that went on between him and the animals brought back too many unpleasant memories. She didn't want to know.

"Come on," Adam said, checking his watch. "Lunch should be ready by now."

When they got back to the Hutchinsons' house, the table was already laid and Roly and Em were rushing around noisily in their impatience to get started.

"At last," Em said as she saw the truck arriving back.

"We'll have none of that," said their mum.

"Have a good morning, Miriam?" she asked, as she and Adam came in.

"It's all very, very impressive," Miriam said. "I had no idea that zoos these days were so . . . so . . . well, animal-orientated."

"It's been a gradual, but very welcome change," Tom admitted. "There's still a lot to do, but we're getting there. Aren't we, Adam?" he added.

"Bit by bit," he nodded.

Soup and rolls were followed by a casserole and rounded off with banana ice-cream. Tom, Ally and Miriam chatted generally about the zoo, about bringing up kids, about the recipe for the soup, about the pros and cons of living in towns or in the country. It was polite and friendly enough, but not what Miriam really wanted to talk to the couple about. Only when Adam took the two kids outside for a game of football, did she finally get round to the question she'd been wanting to ask for the whole meal.

"How *is* Adam?" she asked.

"Well, how does he seem to you?" Tom replied.

"He seems fine," Miriam admitted. "Really happy."

"And I'm sure he is," Ally said. "And we certainly love having him stay with us."

"He's great with the children," Tom said.

"Children and animals," Miriam said thoughtfully. "He's always had a special affinity to them."

"Your son is a remarkable man," Tom said. "I've never come across anyone else in the zoo world with such an overall vision as Adam. He's a planner. Even when I can't see the point of some of his suggestions, everything becomes clear some while later."

"How do you mean?" Miriam asked.

"Well," said Tom, "two examples. When he first came, he was obsessed with the idea of animals becoming bored. It was something we'd never really considered – as long as the animals were clean and well fed, we thought that was enough. But he was quite insistent, and one by one, he invented all these gadgets and devices to keep the animals' minds active."

"One of the weirdest was for the leopards," Ally added. "He said that it was too dull for them simply to be given a lump of meat every day at three, so now, not only are their meal times staggered, but they have to work for their food. The keepers don't just throw the meat through the bars any more. Oh no. Sometimes it's put on a high shelf and the leopard has to leap for it. Other times, and this is done with the other big cats too, it's mounted on to a pulley system and pulled across the enclosure like a running animal."

"Sounds ingenious," Miriam admitted.

"The mongooses and meerkats are given long tubes stuffed with sawdust and maggots," Tom continued. "In-stead of being fed all at once, they have to wait for the maggots to wriggle out through the holes. Much more like them scratching for food in the bark of trees. The chimps have been given all sorts of complicated apparatus to obtain their food and water from, and different mechanisms are used every day. And he's installed tape-recorders playing sounds of another troop next to the gibbon enclosure to give them a bit of company; bears are given salmon to fish for, hives to plunder; the kinkajous' fruit is suspended from string so they have to climb for it. A thousand little changes."

"And does it all work?"

"It seems to," Tom said. "Much as I hate treating animals as though they have human feelings, they really do seem, well . . . *happier* now."

"How can you tell?"

"Oh, it's easy," Ally said. "You never see them obviously disturbed any more: repeating certain gestures over and over; pacing up and down, grooming themselves till all their hair falls out. That sort of thing."

"The *second* thing he's done," Tom added, "is to insist on closer links with other zoos throughout the world. There seems to be a whole group of these talented young men and women who all emerged around the same time."

"All introducing the various new methods of care and supervision," Ally said.

"And all with a strange ability somehow to *communicate* with the animals," Tom added. "It really has to be seen to be believed."

"Oh, I believe it," Miriam said quietly.

"Rather than being mere pleasure parks for an afternoon's entertainment, the zoos have become genuine sanctuaries for animals," Tom explained. "He's taken this zoo by storm, and no mistake," he added. "He'll be head-keeper here before long, despite his age, you mark my words."

Miriam nodded.

Outside, they heard the sudden sound of Adam's truck coughing into action and being revved up. Tom checked his watch.

"Good grief," he said. "Is that the time already?"

"Where's he going?" Miriam asked.

"His last check of the day," Tom said. "He goes out every afternoon after the visitors have left, just to make sure that everything's all right. Would you like to follow him?"

"If we could," Miriam said.

By the time they had climbed up into Tom's truck and set off, Adam was nowhere to be seen.

"Are you sure we'll be able to find him?" Miriam asked. "It's such an enormous place."

"I'm fairly sure I know where he's going," Tom said, driving off towards the central hill. "I remember you once saying he was good with cats and dolphins. If he's where I think he is, you're going to be amazed. Amazed."

Miriam looked out of the window in silence as they drove along the road separating the sections containing the African and Asian animals. Hearing about the achievements of her son, which he'd evidently played right down in his letters to her, she felt totally overawed by the person he'd become. When she thought back to the diagnosis she had been given all those years ago by the specialist at the hospital, and then compared it with Tom's description of him, she was overcome with relief and anger. How dare they have been so wrong?

Before they arrived at the central hill, Tom turned off to the right and parked next to a large field.

"I was right," he said, pointing over to the far side.

Miriam looked and saw a tiny figure galloping around on the back of a massive animal. Her first thought was that it must be a horse, or a camel, or perhaps, given the size, an elephant, but as she looked closer she saw that it was none of these. She gasped.

"Technically speaking, it's totally impossible," Tom said. "Rhinos are the most dangerously bad-tempered animals on earth. And the ones here certainly aren't tame."

"But . . .?" Miriam started to say.

"I've no idea," Tom said. "It's a complete mystery. I thought he'd be here because one of the other rhinos was injured yesterday, but I've seen him riding zebras, antelopes – even pacing around on the back of one of the polar bears. It's not possible, and yet . . ."

As Miriam continued to stare in amazement, she saw her son slip down from the rhino's back. Her heart raced furiously as she watched three of the others trot over to where he was standing. One toss of the head and they could crush him. But it didn't happen. Instead, he stroked their ears and walked out of the field unscathed.

"See what I mean?" Tom said.

"I don't know what to say," Miriam answered.

"They're almost extinct in the wild," he said. "But here they're safe – no one building on their land, no one poisoning their water supply, no one shooting them for their horns. Perhaps they know they won't come to any harm?" he suggested.

Miriam watched her son intently as he climbed over the fence and made for the hill. A shudder tingled down her spine as she remembered the picture of the little boy playing with his wooden Ark for hour after hour. He'd always said he'd like to look after all the animals. It seemed as though he had somehow contrived to do just that.

"What's he doing now?" she asked, as he reached the top of the hill and stood there with his arms outstretched.

Before Tom could answer, the entire zoo echoed with a tumultuous cacophany of animal sound. Miriam jumped nervously. It sounded like a war-cry.

"What on earth was that?" she asked.

"I don't know," Tom admitted. "But it happens every evening as the sun goes down."

What they didn't know, what they couldn't know, was what Adam had been saying to them.

'Good morning,' he'd greeted the waking nocturnal animals. 'Sleep well,' he wished the rest.

Neither Miriam nor Tom were able to hear because unlike Adam, they couldn't communicate through Mammalogue. Mammalogue; the language which had once united all the new tiny mammals as they struggled to survive beside the giant dinosaurs. Mammalogue; which had now brought them all together once again. Through the efforts of the dolphins, they had been snatched from the clutches of extinction just in the nick of time. Rescued from a fate caused by the thoughtlessness of the planet's youngest mammal: human beings.

'When are we going to leave?' Adam called out.

'Tomorrow,' came the reply.

'And where are we going?'

'Home!' they had called back, and all at once the zoo had been filled with the deafening sound of all the animals roaring, trumpeting, barking, bellowing, mewing, chattering and squeaking their approval.

They were familiar questions. The same questions that Adam would ask every evening. The animals knew that it would take a long time before humans learnt to respect the planet. They knew that years would pass before they'd be allowed back to where they belonged. They realized that it

could take decades before men and women came to understand that their own survival depended on the animals they
seemed so intent on destroying.

But in the mean time, here, on their Ark, they could wait
safe and sound until that special tomorrow finally arrived.

Some other Puffins

THE WEATHER WITCH
Paul Stewart

Clee Manor is hardly the kind of place that young Londoners Kerry and Joe want to spend the summer. But as direct descendants of the sixteenth-century witch who was responsible for the disappearance of the village of Cleedale, they find themselves drawn into the house's mysterious past.

It is only when they discover the long-lost village and encounter the Weather Witch herself, however, that they begin to understand the danger and awesome power they face.

A RIVER RAN OUT OF EDEN
James Vance Marshall

Young Eric seeks shelter from a terrible storm which sweeps across the island, and discovers a rare and beautiful gold-furred seal. A warm friendship grows between the boy and the animal, but their friendship is threatened by two men who want to kill the golden seal for her valuable fur. One of the men is Eric's father, whom he loves and trusts; the other is a stranger who plots against Eric's father and tries to come between his parents.

WILD!
Rosalind Kerven

The Rushing family have developed an astonishing rapport with the wild animals who share their remote mountain home. But the beautiful wilderness is about to be destroyed and turned into an enormous theme park. Dave and Emma, their friends from London, are determined to save Old Mountain. And who better to help them than the charismatic pop-star, Wild Man? Soon the campaign reaches national television – and suddenly a lot of accepted ideas about animals are turned upside-down.

RUN SWIFT, RUN FREE

Tom McCaughren

Summer has come to the land of Sinna, and the new foxcubs are growing up. They as yet know nothing of the terrible dangers faced by their parents in recent times, and have much to learn before they can safely fend for themselves.

The final part of this award-winning trilogy, begun with *Run With the Wind* and *Run to Earth*, follows the adventures of the young foxes as a new generation learns to survive in a hostile world, and to run swift, run free.

WHO EVER HEARD OF
A VEGETARIAN FOX?

Rosalind Kerven

Sarah and her sister Caroline both care passionately about animals, but their new home is surrounded by traps and snares set by the gamekeeper and they set about a campaign of sabotage. Then they make friends with Ian, the gamekeeper's son. His arguments for the gamekeeper are just as convincing as Caroline's are against, and Sarah finds herself caught between the two of them.

ENVIRONMENTALLY YOURS
Early Times

What is the greenhouse effect? Why is the Earth getting warmer? Who is responsible for the destruction of the countryside? Where can you get advice on recycling? When will the Earth's resources run out? The answers to all these questions and many more are given in this forthright and informative book. Topics such as transport, industry, agriculture, population and energy are covered as well as lists of 'green' organizations and useful addresses.

ANIMAL KIND
Early Times

Animal Kind looks at what humans are doing to animals. It also looks at what humans *could* be doing for animals to make their lives happier and to lessen their suffering. This is a hard-hitting book that covers topics such as vivisection, vegetarianism, farming, wildlife, pets and blood sports. It will help you look again at your relationship to the animal world.

THE ANIMAL QUIZ BOOK
Sally Kilroy

Why do crocodiles swallow stones? Which bird migrates the furthest? Can kangaroos swim? With over a million species, the animal kingdom provides a limitless source of fascinating questions. In this book Sally Kilroy has assembled a feast for inquiring minds – from domestic animals to dinosaurs, fish to footprints, reptiles to record breakers. Discover where creatures live, how they adapt to their conditions, the way they treat each other, the dangers they face – you'll be surprised how much you didn't know.